Thomas J. Sizer

The Crisis

its rationale

Thomas J. Sizer

The Crisis
its rationale

ISBN/EAN: 9783337378660

Printed in Europe, USA, Canada, Australia, Japan

Cover: Foto ©Andreas Hilbeck / pixelio.de

More available books at **www.hansebooks.com**

ITS RATIONALE.

PART I.—OUR NATIONAL FORCE THE PROPER REMEDY.

PART II.—RESTORATION OF LEGITIMATE AUTHORITY THE
END AND OBJECT OF THE WAR.

BY THOMAS J. SIZER.

BUFFALO:

BREED, BUTLER & CO.

1862.

PREFACE.

A crisis in national affairs is not necessarily measured by days or months. The first part of this endeavor to show the rationale of that through which our nation is passing, was published early in May, 1861. It announced facts and principles that have since been more fully realized. The magnitude of the occasion continues, and reasons similar to those which prompted the first publication seem now to require its extension.

The first part not being temporary in character and purpose, and being introductory to, and closely connected with, what is now added in the second part, it is republished therewith.

It is not supposed by the author that a full statement of the philosophy of this crisis can be embodied in a brief publication; but it is believed that leading principles, being recognized, even though briefly and imperfectly stated, the whole subject may be more easily comprehended and acted on.

The first part was so entirely impersonal, that the author's name seemed immaterial. It being necessary, in the part now added, to treat somewhat of the actors in the history which we are making, remaining anonymous would, perhaps, not be entirely justifiable.

T. J. S.

BUFFALO, June, 1862.

THE CRISIS: ITS RATIONALE.

The time has come for the exposure of a great, and, it may be, a disastrous fallacy in the political reasoning of our people. Regarding *interest* as the controlling power in worldly affairs, the States as sovereign, and that sovereignty referable to the masses of the people in each State, under our republican system, they have assumed that slavery must abide the sure action of the principles of political economy, and live or die, according as enlightened self-interest, acting upon the whole people of each State, influenced by climate and productions, shall determine.

Prominent political men, seeking excuses for inaction or acquiescence, have repeatedly advanced this sedative doctrine; and people of all parties have too readily accepted it as true.

The error consists in overlooking the fact that the interest of the slaveholder is great and permanent, and is not the interest of the State; and that the interest of the State does not control political action. In the case of slavery, republicanism is not permitted to act; the people of the Slave States are not permitted to be enlightened in regard to their interest on the subject, and if they were enlightened, they are not permitted, as against slavery, to control the action of their States. This is not in accordance with the theory and philosophy of our system, but it is our actual condition, and whoever would help our country, in its present crisis, should know it and give it thoughtful heed. The necessities of slavery create for it a political system that is really irreconcilable with our constitutional political system.

The system of government devised by our fathers, is one of most perfect and practical republicanism. It differs from other systems of republicanism, especially in its provisions for great national power and expansion, combined with provisions for complete local self-government, guaranteed against revolutionary

violence. and physical force. Its true character was so well described by Mr. Calhoun,* that his language is copied here, not
only as a clear and correct statement, but also as a valuable
testimony from one whose example and teachings have nevertheless, done much, very much, to defeat the practical working
of our system, according to his own explanation of its nature and
intention. Treating of the guarantees in the Constitution against
external and internal violence towards a State, and against
encroachment by rulers, he says:

"Having now answered your several questions, I deem it due, both to myself
and the occasion, to state in conclusion what, according to the opinion I enter-
tain would be the effects of these guarantees, on the supposition that the Federal
Government shall faithfully discharge the duties they impose.

"The great and leading effect would be, to put an end to all changes in the form of
government and Constitutions of the States, originating in force or revolution : unless,
indeed, they should be effected against the united resistance of the State and the Federal
Government. It would give to the government and constitution of each, the stability of
the whole ; so that no one could be subverted without subverting, at the same time, the
whole system; and this I believe to have been the intention of the framers of the Federal Constitution in inserting the guarantee section. They were experienced and wise
men, and did their work effectually. They had carried the country successfully through,
by their wisdom and patriotism, the most remarkable political revolution on the
records of history, and firmly established the Constitutions and Governments of the
States, composing the Union, on the great principles of popular liberty, in which it
originated. Nothing was left undone to perfect their great and glorious task, but to
reconstruct, on more correct and solid principles, the common Constitution and Government of all the States, and bind them into one compact and durable structure.
This was their crowning work; and how well it was performed, the Federal Constitution and Government will stand more durable than brass, an everlasting monument
of their wisdom and patriotism.

"But very imperfect, indeed, would their task have been left, if they had not
adopted effectual means to guard all the parts against the lawless shocks of violence
and revolution. They were too deeply read in the history of free and confederated
States not to know the necessity of taking effectual guards against them ; and for this
purpose, inserted in the Constitution the guarantee section, which will effectually and
forever guard against those dangerous enemies of popular and constitutional governments, if the Federal Government shall faithfully do its duty. They would, in such
case, effectually close the doors, on every side, against their entrance, — whether attempted by invasion from *without*, domestic violence from *within*, or through the lawless ambition and usurpation of rulers.

"But while the framers of the Federal Constitution thus carefully protected the
system against changes by the rude hand of violence and revolution, they were
too experienced and wise to undertake to close the door against all changes. They
well knew that all the works of man, whatever may be their skill, are imperfect of
themselves, and liable to decay ; and that, in order to perfect and perpetuate what

* See his letter to Hon. William Smith, of Rhode Island, July 3, 1843, in the 6th
vol. of Calhoun's works, p. 234.

they had done, it was necessary to provide a remedy to correct its imperfections and repair the injuries of time, by making such changes as the one or the other might require. They also knew that, if such changes were not permitted, violence and revolution would, in time, burst open the doors which they had so carefully closed against them, and tear down the whole system in their blind and unskillful attempts to repair it. Nor were they ignorant that, in providing for amendments, it would be necessary, in order to give sufficient stability to the system, to guard against hasty and thoughtless innovations, but, at the same time, to avoid such restrictions as would not leave sufficient facility for making the requisite changes. And this too, is executed with the same wisdom and skill which characterized every other part of their work in the various provisions contained in the Federal Constitution for amendments; — which, while they afford sufficient guards against innovations, afford at the same time, sufficient facility for the objects contemplated. But one thing still remained to perfect their work.

"It might be that the party in power would be opposed to all changes, and that, in consequence of the door being thus closed against force and revolution, and the restrictions imposed on the amending power, in order to prevent hasty innovations, —they might make successful resistance against all attempts to amend the constitution, however necessary, if no adequate provision were made to prevent it This they foresaw, and provided against it an ample remedy ; after explaining which, I shall close this long communication.

"The framers of the Federal Constitution were not only experienced and wise men, but firm believers also in the capacity of their fellow-citizens for self-government. It was in the full persuasion of the correctness of this belief that, after having excluded violence and revolution, or physical force as the means of change, and placed adequate guards against innovation, they opened wide the doors — never to be closed — for the free and full operation of all the moral elements in favor of change; not doubting that if reason be left free to combat error, all the amendments which time and experience might show to be necessary, would, in the end be made; and that the system, under their salutary influence, would go on indefinitely, purifying and perfecting itself. Thus thinking,—the liberty of the press,—the freedom of speech and debate,— the trial by jury,— the privilege of *habeas corpus*,— and the right of the people peaceably to assemble together, and petition for a redress of grievances,—are all put under the sacred guarantee of the Federal Constitution, and secured to the citizen against the power both of the Federal and State Governments. Thus it is, that the same high power, which guarantees protection to the governments of the States against change or subversion by physical force, guarantees, at the same time, to the citizens protection against restrictions on the unlimited use of these great moral agents for effecting such changes as reason may show to be necessary. Nor ought their overpowering efficacy to accomplish the object intended, to be doubted. Backed by perseverance and sustained by these powerful auxiliaries, reason in the end will surely prevail over error and abuse, however obstinately maintained; — and this the more surely, by the exclusion of so dangerous an ally as mere brute force. The operation may be slow, but will not be the less sure. Nor is the tardiness an objection. All changes in the fundamental laws of the State, ought to be the work of time, ample discussion, and reflection; and no people who lack the requisite perseverance to go through the slow and difficult process necessary at once to guard against improper innovations, and to insure wise and salutary changes, –or who are ever ready to resort to revolution, instead of reform, where reform may be practicable,—can preserve their liberty. Nor would it be desirable, if it were practicable, to make the requisite changes without going through a long previous process of discussion and agitation. They are indispensable means,--the only school (if I may be allowed the expression,) in our case, that can diffuse and fix in the mind of the community, the principles and doctrines necessary to uphold our complex but beautiful system of governments. In none that ever existed, are they so much required; and in none were they ever calculated to produce such powerful effect. Its very complication — so many distinct sovereign and independent States, each with its separate government, and all united under one — is calculated to give a force to discussion and agitation, never before known, — and to cause a diffusion of political intelligence heretofore unknown in the history of the world.—if the Federal Government shall do its duty under the guarantees of the Constitution by thus promptly suppressing physical force as an element of change, — and keeping wide open the door for the full and free action of all the moral elements in its favor. No people ever had so fair a start. All that is lacking is, that we shall understand in all its great and beautiful proportions the noble political structure reared by the wisdom and patriotism of our ancestors, and to have the virtue and the sense to preserve and protect it."

This is, undoubtedly, the true theory of our government; republicanism guaranteed to every State — the liberty of the press — the freedom of speech and debate — the trial by jury — the privilege of *hab as corpus* — and the right of the people peaceably to assemble together, and petition for a redress of grievances — all put under the sacred guarantee of the Federal Constitution and secured to the citizens against the power both of the Federal and State Governments.

Such is our theory — our system; but such, unfortunately, is not our practice, especially where slavery is concerned. We think it logically demonstrable that slavery cannot permanently coëxist with republicanism thus guaranteed. We think our fathers knew this, and that they expected, when they guaranteed republicanism in the States and did not guarantee slavery there, that republicanism would root out slavery: We think, also, that they who are determined, in every event, to hold on to slavery, are also aware of its real incompatibility with our system, and that to this, are to be ascribed their persevering attempts, first, to change our system by construction, and, failing in this, to withdraw from it with their cherished "institution."

The known necessities of slavery have caused to grow up in these United States, wherever slavery exists, a system utterly at war with our proper system, and with many of the plainest and most important provisions of our Constitution. The liberty of the press, the freedom of speech and debate, do not, and cannot, exist, where slavery is to be permanent. The trial by jury, the privilege of *habeas corpus*, and the right of the people peaceably to assemble together and petition for a redress of grievances, may not be violated by statutory enactments, or judicial construction, in Slave States; but Vigilance Committees and Lynch-law, supersede other law, and provide effectively for the necessities of slavery. The slave laws of Kansas shocked the moral sense of the people, and even of the United States Senate, but their provisions were not worse than the necessities of slavery, existing in such a community, actually require. Such provisions have to be enforced where slavery exists, and the practical result is the same, whether the law is administered according to Judge Lynch, or has a more formal sanction. Judge Lumpkin, of Georgia, expounding the severe provisions of their laws against the education or intellectual employment of negroes, says:

"I do not refer to these severe restrictions for the purpose of condemning them. They have my hearty and cordial approval. The great principle of self-preservation demands, on the part of the white population unceasing vigilance and firmness, as well as uniform kindness, justice and humanity. Everything must be interdicted which is calculated to render the slave discontented with his condition, or would tend to increase his capacity for mischief." *

The great principle of self-preservation demands, on the part of the white population unceasing vigilance and firmness. Every thing must be interdicted which is calculated to render the slave discontented with his condition. This is not only thus authoritatively expounded to be the law and the reason of the law, but it commends itself to our understanding: we see that, in the nature of the case, it must be so, and that slavery, admitted to be permanent, carries with it, by the force of its actual necessities, a system of government and of law adapted to itself and its self-preservation, whatever may be the professed forms of government. From the cautious necessities of slavery, result general popular ignorance, and the concentration of political power in the hands of slaveholders. Their interests become the interests of the State government. They wield the political power, and others share in their favor only as they show themselves acquiescent and serviceable.

Reasoning *à priori* we would infer this state of things; looking at facts we see it exemplified. For more than forty years, States in this Union — not one, only, but a considerable number of them — have been shown to be held down and impoverished by slavery. Lying side by side with other States free from slavery, yet having no better soil or climate or natural productiveness, the general and aggregate wealth of the people and their standard of living are seen to be vastly inferior to those of the Free States. There stands the fact, too patent for denial or equivocation. Yet not in one of these States is that law of self-interest which is so much relied on, working, however gradually, the extinction of slavery. Surely if the law were so potent, forty years are long enough for it to begin to act. Obviously it is not true that slavery will be abandoned when it becomes unprofitable to *a State*, or to *the people* of a State; because the republican system contemplated by our fathers, and guaranteed by the Constitution, does not prevail in the Slave States, but is overborne and crushed out there by the despotic necessities of slavery. Hence it is, that, gradually, there has grown up in the Slave States, a systematic distrust of majorities. More and more their State Constitutions have guarded against popular influences, especially where slavery is concerned : and Mr. Calhoun, during the latter part of his life, expressed frequent apprehension and dread of what he called " the tyranny of majorities," and gave much attention to contriving methods whereby the minority might check and control the majority.

The example of some States that did actually abolish slavery, will, perhaps, be cited as against our reasoning, but it is not. Slavery in those States had not yet attained the political control, and men were then nearer to the times and more imbued with the spirit of the revolution. Republicanism was not then suppressed, but was active and dominant in those States, according to the true intent and meaning of the Constitution. Freedom of discussion and the interest of the masses prevailed over the interest and desires of the slaveholders. If any of the latter favored the movement it was because their sense of right or their other interests overcame their interests as slaveholders. Had the question been left to the slaveholders in those States, *their* interest would never have led them to abolish slavery. It was the interest of the masses sustained by their moral convictions, enacting and enforcing positive legal prohibitions, against the interests and wishes of slaveholders, that abolished slavery in those States ; and not the changed interests or relaxing cupidity of the slaveholders themselves. Where slaveholders have the political power, slavery will never be abolished, whatever may be its impoverishing effects on the State or the masses of the people ; and this law will prevail whatever the climate or the productions of the State. The law of interest does not work there, through the masses, to abolish slavery, but through the slaveholders, to perpetuate it.

The interest of the slaveholder in his slave is, always and everywhere, precisely measured by the marketable pecuniary value of the slave—by his price. Where a slave can be sold for fifty dollars, that fact signifies that, in that case, slavery, or the right or legal ability to hold the person in bondage, is actually worth fifty dollars to the master. So if the price be ten dollars, or five thousand dollars, the price measures the marketable value to the master, of the relation between him and his bondman. And therefore, wherever a slave will sell *for anything,* slavery is valuable to the master, and therefore his interest will not lead him to abolish it. There is no part of the United States in which slavery, or the unlimited right of one man to appropriate the services of another, would not be pecuniarily and largely valuable. The colored people of Chicago would, if held there as slaves, constitute a large pecuniary interest of their owners. The legal right and ability to work a gang of stalwart fugitives in the Canadian forests, would insure a fortune there, to their master: and Gov. Wise was right when he told us of the great pecuniary value of slaves to dig for gold in California, if only slavery were legalized and protected there. Some pertinent statements and statistics are copied here, from the letter of an intelligent observer who was traveling in Kentucky.* He says:

"It is a common assertion that the complete substitution of free labor for slave labor would be profitable, and that even without Abolition action and outside pressure, such change would be produced, in a somewhat longer time, by the choice of the slaveholders, directed by considerations of economy. There is no proposition more groundless. If free labor was more cheap and profitable, many slaveholders would have learned it, and have already made the complete substitution. This has not occurred, as I am informed, on a single farm in Kentucky, unless where the easy access of Abolitionist negro-stealers renders the holding of slaves too hazardous. If any reliance really were placed in this often-asserted dogma, the certain result would have been seen in a great diminution of the number of slaves, and even remote from the Abolition border, compared to the whites. On the contrary, the proportion of slaves has been increased, and greatly, from the census of 1790 to the last of 1850—and regularly to 1840. The small relative diminution between 1840 and 1850, (though still with an absolute increase in that time of 28,723 slaves), may safely be ascribed, and entirely, to the incendiary action of Northern Abolitionists, and not, in the least,

* His letter is dated at Frankfort, Ky., and was published in the Charleston Mercury, Sept. 24, 1860.

to negro slavery being otherwise less profitable. The proportions in Kentucky have been very nearly as follows:

"1790, there was one slave to every five white inhabitants.

"1800, there was one slave to every four and a half white inhabitants.

"1810, there was one slave to every four white inhabitants.

"1820, there was one slave to every three and a half white inhabitants.

"1830, there was one slave to every three white inhabitants.

"1840, there was one slave to every three white inhabitants.

"1850, there was one slave to every three and a half white inhabitants.

"If the smaller proportional increase of slaves in the last cited decade was caused by diminution of their economical value, (if not affected by Abolition action), it becomes those who maintain that general proposition to show what difference has occurred in the agriculture of Kentucky, or otherwise, to produce such change of value in labor. In truth, there are few, if any agriculturists, and none in this better portion of Kentucky, who do not use, or would not prefer, slaves to hired free laborers—as would be the case, if the choice were free, in every now free State where the climate is as mild. And if fanaticism and legal prohibition and penalties did not prevent the holding of negro slaves, and their secure and quiet possession anywhere, they would be bought and held in numbers, and to great advantage, for menial employments and as house servants, in every now non-slaveholding State, without regard to severity of climate. At least, all wealthy house-keepers would rejoice to own negro slaves as domestic servants, to save their wives and daughters from their present toil and drudgery, in acting as servants, and performing all the most revolting, degrading, and debasing duties of such service.

"Negro slavery is nowhere now kept out of either the new Territories, or the older Northern States, by its being unprofitable for every employment; but is excluded by positive prohibitory laws and penalties, and still more by the prevailing anti-slavery fanaticism, which alone would render property in slaves entirely insecure and worthless, and make the possessor odious in the highest degree. If negro slaves could be taken to, and held securely under the laws in any State or Territory, where the profit or convenience of owners would require, they would spread into every Northern State, and be demanded in such numbers, that a million of slave population, to be there held, would not more than maintain the needed supply. The most earnest advocates for the advantages of the institution of negro slavery, and for its greatest extension, would ask no better means for the desired ends, than the fair and full application of the rule of leaving the demand for slaves, and the profits of their employment, with their secure possession, to direct and limit their use, and to determine the extension and limits of the institution of negro slavery."

To this testimony we add, (what all must know), that the vices and passions of men contribute largely to sustain slavery everywhere; and also that, contrary to general impression, the Census shows* the expectation of life of colored persons to be greater in New England than in Louisiana.

We think the observations above quoted substantially correct, and that the pecuniary interest of slaveholders can nowhere be relied on to relax human bondage. If *they* control the State, the

* See abstract of U. S. Census, 1850, p. 13.

Government expresses and responds to their interests. Slavery, originated and sustained by cupidity, nowhere subsides of its own accord. Only the adverse interests and moral convictions of non-slaveholders, armed with legal power, can reach and abolish it. Slaveholders know this, instinctively, and hence they grasp and hold instinctively to political power; and hence, in no slave State, can the system of enlightened popular self-government, provided for by the Constitution and so justly described by Mr. Calhoun, be permitted to prevail. The peculiar, self-constituted, oligarchical system established by slavery, must prevail there instead; and even the provisions of the Constitution, where they conflict with it, must, of necessity, give way.

But the spirit of the age and the moral sense of mankind, aided by the press, the telegraph and railroads, are dangerous to the continued political supremacy of slavery in the slave States, even when aided by its self-constituted and unconstitutional anti-republican system. The several slave States actually need, for the safe perpetuation of their system, the effective protection of a national government. Slavery, with all its advantages guaranteed by State constitutions, and the increasing stringency of its system of influence, terror, and power, is, in itself, so essentially weak and wrong, that it actually needs, and must have, strong, positive, and active support and protection from a government armed with national power. Therefore, politicians in the slave States, and their allies and coadjutors, have not been engaged in a work of supererogation, when seeking, in every possible way, by construction and otherwise, to press our general government into the active service of slavery, and to save slavery from even the possible influence of republicanism in the slave States.

Hon. Albert Rust, member of Congress from Alabama, said in his place last fall:

"It is only by denying to legislative bodies everywhere under our government, the power to impair or affect the right of property in slaves, that you give permanent peace and security to the slaveholder."

The Committee on Federal Relations in the South Carolina Legislature, last fall, said:

"Out of the Union, our means and resources will go to build up a power under our own control, to be wielded by ourselves for our defence."

Gov. Pettus, of Mississippi, in his message to the Legislature, in special session, (Nov. 26, 1860), said, referring to the past, it had been the opinion of many,

"That we might still defend ourselves in the Union, by the power of our State governments, *with the aid of the Federal Government.* But when, in a recent presidential election, a large majority have decreed that *the Federal Government, with all its immense power on which we relied for protection,* shall hereafter be administered by the same class of men who have been guilty of all these acts of violence and bad faith, it is folly, it is madness, to hope for safety in such a government."

The sentences we have italicised, show the point for which the quotation is given.

Mr. Rhett, of South Carolina, a prominent leader in the secession movement, and when just elected to the Convention, said. (Nov. 12, 1860):

"The Southern Confederacy, ought to be a Slaveholding Confederacy. It is *no* experiment that free government should exist in slaveholding countries. The Republics of Rome and Greece—still the light and glory of ancient times—were built on domestic slavery. But it *is* an experiment to maintain free government with universal suffrage, and the whole population to control the government.

"Population increases faster than capital, and no prosperity can long stave off the dire conflict which must arise between want and affluence—population and capital. Where the great majority of the population have no *property,* which is the case with every nation in Europe, what shall protect property under the control of this majority from partition or confiscation? What is liberty worth with starvation; and what is property worth with confiscation? Our Confederacy must be a Slaveholding Confederacy. We have had enough of a confederacy with dissimilar institutions."

Vice-President Stephens, in a speech lately, at Atlanta, Georgia, where he had a public reception, speaking of their new Constitution, said:

"The changes in our Constitution were made with a view to conform to our social institutions, and afford a greater protection to our slave property."

Thus, looking into the real reason of our present difficulties, it is found in *the necessities of slavery for active national protection* —an inherent incongruity between Slavery and Republicanism— between the system which slavery necessitates, and the system guaranteed by our Federal Constitution. It is the irrepressible conflict; and the Sphynx-question now propounded to us, is,— which shall prevail, Slavery and its now recognized necessities, or, the Republican government founded by our fathers, and established by our Constitution?

Let us not be misunderstood. We are not presenting immediate abolition as the alternative, much less are we suggesting that the Federal Government should, in any way whatever, engage in the abolition of slavery in the States. For aught we have said, and for aught that appears, slavery may continue for years, and for generations, as it has continued in the Slave States, subject only to the rightful action of moral and political influences in the States themselves. While it can fairly meet and deal with these, let it live, and, if it can, flourish. When it cannot do so—and we believe that permanently and successfully it cannot—there is now no government, and there never should be any, to put down republicanism in the States, in order to sustain slavery there. Our Constitution guarantees the perpetuity of republicanism there, and it does not guarantee the perpetuity of slavery. We believe the Constitution is right; and if slavery, anxiously forecasting, determines now to set up its ultimate necessities as paramount to the Constitution, then the Government and the Constitution, and not Slavery, are to be sustained.

That the subversion of our Republican system has long been deliberately purposed and planned, we have had abundant evidence, but did not sufficiently believe it. That leading southern journal, the *Richmond Enquirer*, said, about the 1st of September, 1856 :

"The election of Mr. Buchanan may, and probably will, originate a reaction in public opinion that will encourage the extension of the conservative institution of slavery, and the extension of the British and southern European races, for the very purpose of stemming and turning back the torrent of infidelity, materialism, sensuality, agrarianism, and anarchy, that threatens to overwhelm us from the prolific hive of northern Europe.

"The election of Mr. Buchanan would be a reactionary movement in favor of slavery and conservatism.

"'Forewarned, forearmed.' We see the numbers, the character, the designs of our enemies. Let us prepare to resist them and drive them back.

"Let the South present a compact and undivided front. Let her show to the barbarians that her sparse population offers but little hopes of plunder ; her military and self-reliant habits, and her firm union and devoted resolution, no chance of conquest. Let her, if possible, detach Pennsylvania and southern Ohio, southern Indiana, and southern Illinois, from the North, and make the highlands between the Ohio and the lakes the dividing line. Let the South treat with California, and, if necessary, ally herself with Russia, with Cuba, and Brazil.

"A common danger from without, and a common necessity (slavery) within, will be sure to make the South a great, a united, a vigilant, and warlike people."

The same paper, in a subsequent article, (Oct. 14, 1856), after carefully counting up the military resources of Virginia, says:

"Add to this abundant provison of war muniments, the fruits of her certain seizure of Fortress Monroe with its well stored arsenals, as well as the federal armory at Harper's Ferry, on the first occurrence of hostilities with the North ; and her military preparations would be very far from contemptible.　The skill of her people with the rifle and in horsemanship is proverbial ; and we speak the words of calm reflection when we say, in no spirit of boastfulness, that if the North should undertake to invade the South, by throwing open her ports to free trade with foreign nations, and refusing to allow federal duties to be collected in her waters, Virginia could alone drive back their forces.

" Virginia makes no boasts of these preparations ; but as surely as the sun shines over her beautiful fields, she will treat the election of an abolition candidate as a breach of the treaty of 1789, and a release of every sovereign State in the South from all part and lot in its stipulations.　The South will then revert to free trade, her favorite and long-desired policy ; and her commerce will be no longer shackled with a tribute of $50,000,000 to $75,000,000 in annual revenues, which constitute the grand federal corruption fund, to grasp which is the whole object of the abolition agitation, and which has proved itself the 'root of all the evils' which afflict the country."

These statements made more than four years ago, but, we presume, not generally believed then, can, perhaps, better be appreciated now, when the line of policy indicated, is so nearly followed out.　Quotations, of like character, could easily be multiplied.

A reaction to encourage slavery, was then, not only desired but hoped and expected.　" A common danger"—that is, from the people—"and a common necessity (slavery)" were preparing the Slave States for the destruction of our republican system of government, and the establishment of a more "conservative" system — that is, one better guarded against the influence and power of the people — to wit, the oligarchical system of slavery The " infidelity" alluded to, doubtless means the want of faith in slavery as a Christian institution, the "materialism " and " agrarianism" so much dreaded, means, the regard for popular thrift and industry, favored by republicanism, and by "anarchy" is intended, government by the people, and the absence of arbitrary control over them, by an oligarchy of masters.　To obviate these dangers to slavery, to revolutionize a government which acknowledges and guarantees the right of the people to control it, was already a settled purpose.　Confident of the absolute political control of " the South " by the slave interest, it already looked to the consolidation of its power.　"Military habits," " firm union and devoted resolution," not reason, argument or justice were, even then, relied on to carry the day against the people, to overthrow our government, and to establish and perpetuate "the conservative institution" of slavery.

The successive steps in the progress to this point, from the republican theory and system, have been natural and orderly. First, the jealous anxiety of slavery for national control, as manifested in its avidity for Federal offices, and in its acquisition of Slave Territory and exclusion of Free Territory ; then the proposition to secure for itself, by constitutional amendment, a perpetual and equal share in the control of the general government, by means of a dual executive, etc.; then its demand for the abrogation of all Federal restrictions on its extension and for protective federal legislation ; and, finally, failing in these, revolution, to attain its purposes.

We can, now, perhaps, better understand the true character of our present political crisis, and can see how fallacious it must be, to look for remedies in popular action, according to the provisions of our Constitution, *in States where slavery has political control.* The time for such action there, is past. As well might we look for it, in any other despotic or oligarchical government. The necessities of slavery are in the full tide of successful domination there, and necessity knows no other law — no other Constitution. This shows us why, *in every State where slavery has control of the State Government, and so has installed itself as the government* DE FACTO, *no appeal to the people is allowed, where it would be attended with the least risk to slavery, or the revolution which it contemplates.* People there, voters, according to their existing constitutions, even a majority of them, may be really unwilling to be precipitated into revolution. *They cannot help it.* Government is taken away from them — never to be restored, till slavery again yields to the Federal Constitution, and to rightful popular sovereignty in the States. This, it will not, for the present, do. It will only yield to a greater necessity ; and this fact we may better understand first, than last. Republican reasoning, in those States, is utterly vain ; for they who believe in it there, have now no political power, and they who have the political power, do not believe in republicanism, and understand, full well, what they are about, and that, to accomplish their purposes, popular control, except when maddened into hostility to its real interests, must not be permitted. They mean revolution, the supremacy of slavery, and a government better adapted than ours, to its necessities ; and we have no right now, to await, or idly to calculate on, the recuperative action of republicanism according to our Constitution, in the States which slavery has already successfully paralyzed. Murmurs of popular discontent, and even indignant denunciations, against the revolutionists, which now occasionally reach us, from the people of those States, are louder now, than they ever will be again, if the friends, in those States, to our government and our republican system, receive no outside support. Like the cries of shipwrecked sufferers, the popular murmurs there, will grow less and less. Even Austrian despotism relinquishes nothing that it can successfully hold. American despotism is, at least, equally intelligent and regardful of its interests ; and, we believe too, it is equally remorseless. Not right, not constitutional law, not superior power, is arrayed against our government, nor even an excited temporary and local popular enthusiasm, which will cool of itself; but calculating, interested cupidity and ambition, understanding their own purposes and bent on their accomplishment, regardless alike, of popular rights and constitutional provisions. In nature and essence, it is the same power, and governed by the same motives, as that which, in every age of the world, has contemned the people, and trampled on their rights.

Agencies are not wanting here, for its purposes. The very means designed to guard popular liberty, are, when perverted, the most efficient for its destruction. Hon. James Guthrie, of Kentucky, quotes from a Georgia paper :

"We know as well as any one living that the whole movement for secession and the formation of a new government, so far at least as Georgia is concerned, proceeded on only a *quasi* consent of the people, and was pushed through, under circumstances of great excitement and frenzy, by a fictitious majority. With all the appliances brought to bear, with all the fierce rushing, maddening events of the hour, the election of the 4th of January showed a falling off in the popular vote of 25,000 or 30,-000 : and on the night of that election the co-operationists had a majority, notwithstanding the falling off, of nearly 3000, and an absolute majority of elected delegates of 79. But, upon assembling, by wheedling, coaxing, buying, and all the arts of deception, the Convention showed a majority of 31 against Governor Johnson's proposition.

"And thus," says Mr. Guthrie, "went one State out of the Union — against the voice of the people who elected the delegates to the Convention ! Now it is said that a majority of the popular vote of Alabama was cast against going out, but it so chanced that a small majority of the delegates were for secession while the bulk of the people were opposed to it, and they took Alabama out, and refused to let the people have any voice in the matter. The vote of Louisiana too was against secession, but the delegates suppressed it and took Louisiana out against the wishes of the people."

Conventions of the people, the legitimate purpose of which, is, to make governments more conformable to the popular will, are made the most efficient means for depriving the people of political power, and removing it permanently out of their reach. Practically they are coming to be used, as other governmental agencies have been used, from time immemorial, by the few to oppress the many. Somewhere in every political system, there is assumed to be an embodied expression of sovereign power. Sovereignty, admitted to reside with the people, is supposed to be embodied in convention by delegation, and thence it has been too readily assumed that the political powers of a convention are unlimited and absolute. A little reflection must show to every one, the very great danger of this assumption. Grant it, and nothing more is needed, in order to subvert and revolutionize free government, than to get control, by whatever means, of the organization of a convention. Its power is assumed to be illimitable, its sessions indefinite, its edicts supreme. Initiated by the legislature, it determines the manner of constituting future legislatures, and so may secure perpetuity for any system which it chooses to inaugurate. Future legislatures, acting in the same interest, will not call future conventions, except at such times and in such manner as still further to promote and secure the same interest ; and even if the convention should assume to extinguish the legislature, where would be the remedy ? How available are these instrumentalities for the utter subversion of all popular government, was exemplified in the case of Kansas, and the Lecompton Constitution. It is also exemplified now, by the revolutionary State Conventions.

Popular liberty cannot survive the unchecked operation of this system. Delegates to a convention are not themselves sovereign, but only the servants of the real sovereigns, and submission of their action, to the deliberate judgment of the sovereign people, is not only an act of proper respect for the supreme power, but a check upon the exercise of delegated power, the use of which, the people can, with no safety, forego. If, in times past, the informal sanction of the people has, in some instances, been deemed sufficient, with no propriety can the precedent be held to authorize the denial of their right of adoption or rejection in every case. The

2

right is, in the nature of the case, inherent and indestructible. To deny, to circumscribe, or to defeat it, is usurpation, and rebellion against the sovereign power.

When the United States Constitution had been formed, it was submitted to the people of the States for their approval or rejection. They approved it. But the real significance of this act is overlooked, by those who now assume to withdraw legally by *State* Convention. A State Convention has no such power; because this power is, by the compound form of government thus adopted, conferred upon *United States* Conventions, or upon the bodies authorized to act as substitutes therefor. It will be noted that, in either of the legitimate methods of exercising such power, the people would have two opportunities of passing upon such action, and by two sets of their delegates. As Mr. Calhoun has shown in his careful consideration of the Rhode Island case, the people's sovereignty is not to be exercised informally, but is only authoritative, when exercised according to the rules which they have prescribed for themselves. The people of the several States, having, with due formality, prescribed to themselves how they will amend or modify their relations in, or with, the United States Government, cannot, except by revolution, do this, in any other way. The assumption of such power by a *State* Convention, is in derogation of the sovereignty of the people of its own State, as well as of the people of other States affected thereby. Yet we have seen, in several of the Slave States, such power usurped by State Conventions, and we also see them still further exercising their pretended sovereignty, by forming, adopting, officering, and putting in operation, a national government, without reference to the people. The theory evidently is, that sovereignty is in the State Conventions, not in the people. And there is no power in these States to resist enforcement of the theory, because the State Governments are dominated by slavery, and not by the people; and hence it is vain to anticipate effective reaction of republicanism in these States.

But another, and perhaps even a greater, difficulty lies back of this. The people of these States are themselves, already, to an alarming extent, debauched and corrupted by slavery. They are not bred to reason and justice, to a knowledge of, and respect for, human rights, to self-restraint and self-government, but, to a reverence for power, and to the exercise of force. Men who will, in crowds, maltreat a lone, unresisting clergyman, school-teacher, or woman, do not act under the influence of reason, humanity, or regard for legal rights. We do not mean to suggest that they are worse by nature than other people, but that their interest, as they understand it, leads them to sustain slavery, and to sanction whatever is seen to be necessary for its support and perpetuation. During all their lives they have been in the habit of seeing the owners of slaves rise to wealth, power and respectability, and their own hopes point in the same direction, as naturally as do those of a laborer in a Free State, to the ownership of a farm. Cheap negroes and the uninterrupted use of them, are the hope for which they are willing to sacrifice republican principles, and — if sure of success — to fight.

If slavery, having the absolute control of the State Governments in the Slave States, having also largely corrupted the people there, deems, now, that its necessities require a national government specially adapted and devoted to its protection and perpetuation, if it recognizes that our Federal Constitution does not provide such a government, and that slavery can no longer use it as such, — what shall prevent slavery from destroying our present government, and establishing, by revolution, a national government adapted to its necessities and purposes?

Before answering this question directly, we will first indicate what, in our opinion, will certainly *not* prevent it.

We have shown that the people of the Slave States will not, unaided, prevent it, through the action of their State governments — that slavery controls those governments, and is using them, and will probably continue to use them, as governments *de facto*, for the accomplishment of its revolutionary purposes, and that no reactionary influences among the people there, can reasonably be relied on, to arrest the present progress of events.

Considerations of economy — the pecuniary burdens, taxes and expenses of the revolution, will not arrest its progress. The habits of thought and action, in the Slave States, on this subject, are not like those of the people of the Northern, Eastern and Middle States. Such considerations are not so potent there, and, calculations in regard to them are not so closely made, and therefore it is not reasonable to expect them to influence, so decidedly, their public action. Moreover, the actual pecuniary profits of slavery are so great as really and reasonably to warrant, (those profits only considered), a large expenditure for its security. We give some statistics:

Col. Woodson, speaking in Charleston, S. C., concerning Kansas, in March, 1856, said:

"Slaves were worth $1500 each. Upon the above estimates their annual products would reach $910 each, which would give 10 per cent. on the investment, $100 for food and clothing, and $505 clear profit to each hand."

About the same time, a writer in a Florida paper gives, as an instance,

"One planter who works twenty-seven field-hands, counting girls and boys twelve years old, with which he runs twelve plows and plants 250 acres of Sea Island cotton and 175 acres of corn. We suppose it takes the corn to feed the mules and 'people,' and we suppose the cotton will yield 300 pounds per acre; that it is worth 25 cents per pound, making $18,750 for the earnings of 27 slaves, counting boys and girls over twelve years old."

These profits are not so large as some that we have seen stated on apparently good authority, and connected with other branches of slave labor. We see that the pecuniary value of 4,000,000 slaves, at $500 each, is $2,000,000,000.

The Secretary of the Treasury of South Carolina lately estimated the taxable property in that State, thus: Slaves, $270,000,000; land, $105,000,000; all other property, $73,000,000.

Slavery is certainly an enormous pecuniary interest, and therefore large sacrifices can be afforded, for what that interest may be supposed to require.

We are not speaking of the general interest of the whole people, in the Slave States, but only of the pecuniary interest of slavery— the ruling power. Despotisms and oligarchies are generally exceedingly unprofitable to the people, but they are not unprofitable to the rulers themselves, and therefore they are never relinquished by those rulers, from prudential reasons. The House of Hapsburg have flourished, though the nation suffered. *Delirant reges, plectuntur Achivi.* The ambitious political men, who now control, in those States, are reckless of expense; their necessities require them to go on, and probably they may be pecuniarily and largely benefited, though the people and the country should be ruined thereby. Equally reckless are the poor masses, who have nothing to loose, and think they have much to hope from the revolution. Add, also, the expectation (reasonable, perhaps, until lately,) that the expenses of accomplishing the revolution had mostly already been incurred, and the promises, so fascinating to the young, of an independent career of Southern conquest and national glory, and we see how futile are any expectations that the revolution is now to be arrested by dread of the expense, however great may be the real loss and impoverishment of the people or the nation thereby.

The low Southern tariff might, however, if permitted to operate, at the same time withdraw Northern trade, and reimburse the revolutionary exchequer, and, through this means, secession, instead of entailing a discouraging expense, might really bring pecuniary profit and encouragement.

Interference by other nations will not prevent the consummation of the revolution. Less than formerly are European nations inclined to interfere, to prevent revolutions, even on their own continent ; and their motives to do so are less here, especially when, as in this case, the proposed revolution is anti-popular, and favorable to aristocracy—perhaps, to an empire. Unfortunately, also, the promised policy of the proposed government, is really more friendly to their mercantile interests, than that of our present government, and, in this respect, wiser for all concerned. That European nations will recognize, and negotiate with, the "Southern Confederacy" or Empire, if it is permitted to become a national government *de facto*, no one can rationally refuse to believe. Europe has no such interest in the preservation or restoration of our present national government, as we ourselves have ; and, if we acquiesce in its dismemberment and the establishment of another, rival, and, probably, hostile government, on our own borders, and even out of our own territory, how exceedingly pusillanimous and absurd it is to calculate that Europe will, to discourage slavery, and out of a general regard for humanity, veto the rising government, and thus do for us what we will not do for ourselves ! Europe has not extinguished Turkey, Spain, Cuba or Brazil.

Returning affection for the Union, in the Slave States, will not stay the revolution. Were it sufficient for this, the revolution so long contemplated, would never have been begun. Neither is "returning reason" of those people, to be relied on. Their revolutionary movement is no temporary excitement, but is the logical result of sentiments and purposes long entertained and deliberately pondered. "Returning reason" may, however, do good, in at last showing loyal people how to meet the revolutionists.

National considerations — the sense of security, and pride in being part of a great and powerful nation — will not suffice to restore the disaffected. This generation of our people have grown up with this sense of security so strong, that it seems to them to be personal, rather than national, and nothing, perhaps, but a reversed experience, can teach them its source and its value. Besides, if a revolution can be so easily and suddenly accomplished, it may seem that our sense of security was fallacious, and that our national government has not really deserved the confidence and respect it has enjoyed. We cannot shut our eyes, too, to the fact that to the southward over the whole Continent, are rich countries and weak governments inviting to conquest, and that the rivalries, and perhaps hostilities, with the "Northern Republic," may afford are agreeable stimulus to those sentiments of patriotism, which delight to express themselves in action. Looking at this subject, too, from a Southern point of view, as we are now doing, it is not, perhaps, unreasonable to contemplate the gradual and ultimate absorption of all the States into the more plucky and daring, and therefore successful, government, which it is proposed, by means of the revolution, to inaugurate.

Conciliating the border Slave States, by concessions to slavery, will not win back the seceding States, but must, while the separation continues, demoralize the Free States. The most vicious and corrupting influence in our politics is, "the balance of power," or "third party." Only in respect to the slave trade, are the interests of slavery, in the border Slave States, different from its interests in the more Southern States. The border Slave States have probably secured, by their position, the guaranty in the Constitution of the "Southern Confederacy" against the opening of the foreign slave trade. It cannot be doubted that, on the same principle, favorable guarantees will be obtained by them from the Free States. A slave confederacy being permitted on one side of them, ever solicitous for their alliance, and the example of successful secession being before them, nothing but constant acquiescence in their wishes, assiduous cultivation of their interests, and a liberal share of the benefits and emoluments of government, could retain them in the Union. The system of "compromise" would become perpetual, and more one-sided than ever. Soon, perhaps, the "Northern Free Confederacy" would thus become more theoretically and governmentally pro-slavery, than the "Southern Slave Confederacy." What, then, should prevent the union of the two confederacies—in, short, reconstruction of the Union on the slavery basis? The same result would also be attained by a general compromise, satisfactory to slavery.

Such seems the prospect before us, on the principle of *conciliating the border Slave States.* If we refuse to do so, or if we show ourselves, in their estimation, at all niggardly, in our concessions in favor of slavery, they join the new national government to be established for slavery, and find there, that which politicians have, for years, been educating them to consider a *sine qua non*—protection for slavery. For we must not suppose that the interests of slavery are really and greatly inconsistent in the slave-raising and the slave-consuming States. The owner of a gang of slaves in Georgia has as much benefit from the monopoly caused by prohibiting the foreign slave trade, as the owner of a large family of slaves in Virginia; and the non-slaveholders in Virginia might be nearly as much benefited by the cheapening of slaves, through the restoration of the foreign slave trade, as the non-slaveholder of Georgia. Not those who have slaves, anywhere, but those who want them everywhere, would be benefited.

While actual slaveholders control the "Southern Confederacy" it will probably not open the slave trade, however favorable they may be to free trade in articles which they have not. A "slave Republic" might, and indeed ought, logically, to open this trade; but a slave oligarchy or despotism would be more likely to connive at it, as in Cuba and Brazil.

Dread of servile insurrection will not stay the revolution. Ultimately these will certainly come, if slavery has its way ; and in case of a general war, they may, indeed, burst out speedily, and, like the burning barracks in Fort Sumter, slavery may thus smother its defenders. But dread of this, is not yet imminent in the Slave States. It is the custom there, to attribute insurrections to "northern abolitionists," rather than to man's inherent desire for liberty ; and the exclusion of northern men, and extensive military preparations, create, probably now, a sense of increased security from insurrections, except, perhaps, along the borders of the Free States.

Moreover, it is not easy for people bred in the Free States to realize the mastery which strong wills exert over strong men bred to unconditional submission. That free negroes make good soldiers, was shown by the colored regiments which did good service in our war for independence; but it is not the least of the terrible afflictions of slavery, that it so far destroys manhood. It was one of the mistakes of John Brown, that he calculated on the prompt aid of those whom he meant to assist. The terrible penalties sure to fall on resistance, the difficulty of combination and organization by slaves, the facilities for them on the part of the whites, the investigation by torture, the certainty of exposure, through some avenue for strong personal affections, and the unvarying character of experience, make slave insurrections very rare, always of limited extent, and speedily suppressed. Indeed, it may reasonably be supposed that such experience, in this direction, as the governing class, in the Slave States, have had, has strengthened, rather than diminished, their self-confidence. Apprehensions of their inability to create and maintain independent government, if they exist at all, do not arise from within.

Judging, also, with unprejudiced eyes, the prospect that, if our government permits, the revolutionists can not only maintain an independent national government, but greatly extend and strengthen it, justifies the confidence they express. The experiment of the few governing the many, by military rule, is neither new nor unsuccessful. In many respects the conditions are exceedingly favorable for it now, in the Slave States. The proclivity of their educated men, for political employment, is proverbial. It has been indulged and cultivated for generations, by our general government. Our military and naval schools have, also, been most freely and extensively used by them. The degradation of labor, by means of slavery, has caused a large body of poor whites to grow up in idleness, and fitted for nothing so well as to be converted into soldiers. Organization, the great element of power among civilized men, is easier accomplished among a few, and under the consolidating pressure of a strong common interest. Southward, indefinitely, are rich countries with weak governments, and adapted to the evident purposes of the revolutionists, the acquisition of which would give employment to the ambitious and restless, and, at the same time, consolidate and extend their national power.

Waiting for something to turn up, will not stop the revolution. We have waited— waited astonishingly—and still the revolution went on. Very naturally and very regularly it went on. Its conductors have evidently been in earnest, and working with a purpose and a plan. Does a falling body arrest itself? Neither will slavery arrest itself—especially if rushing, unresisted, towards a long-cherished purpose.

What will stop it, and the revolution which it has initiated?— again we ask, and now we answer,—*force, greater force*, nothing but *a greater force*.

With conscious anxiety, slavery has, from the beginning, protested against force ; and its friends and allies, everywhere catching at the word, have promptly echoed "*no coercion;*" and the politicians, accustomed to receive the law from slavery, flying to "compromise," their favorite panacea, and producing each his separate plan, have, nevertheless, shaken their heads with wonderful unanimity, enjoining *peace, peace,* "*no coercion.*" It is one of the shrewdest of all the devices of slavery, thus to impose on the people of a great, strong nation, a pre-determination not to use *the only remedy which slavery really dreads.* Slavery originates in force, it believes in force, it relies upon force, and it only stays its hand where greater force is met or expected. Having determined on revolution, it naturally guarded most, against the use of what it knew would be the most effective preventive. Pretexts were of course needed, and were used liberally. Failure to deliver up escaped slaves, personal liberty laws, exclusion from the territories, &c., &c., were much talked of ; but, that they were only pretexts, was shown by the steady, and even accelerated, onward progress of the revolution, while Congress, in alarm, was appointing committees, and politicians and parties were vieing with each other, in alacrity, to devise remedies for the pretended grievances. And yet, through the whole, and while the revolution was advancing with its utmost speed, through State after State, while emissaries (we may not call them conspirators, for they acted openly,) were freely and frequently passing to and fro, negotiating not only with State, but with Federal authorities, cultivating, preparing and forwarding the revolution, in every possible manner, and with the greatest possible haste,—while arms, public moneys, forts, vessels, and armies were seized everywhere, except where strong resistance was expected, this great, strong, rich, and courageous nation was, while its own dissolution and destruction were progressing, magnetized into quiescence, by the constant warning and threat, that *resistance would precipitate the revolution!* Force, our rightful constitutional, national *force*, and that only, would have stopped it, at any point hitherto—will stop it now.

The extensive general powers of our State governments favor such a revolution, unless our National government *act* in its appropriate sphere. It only needs that State governments should assume national powers, and the General Government acquiesce in such assumption, and the revolution is accomplished. But it is perfectly easy, always, for our General Government to exercise its national functions ; as easy, at least, as for any other national government to exercise such. When it does not exercise them, no defect is chargable upon our system. The whole blame, in such case, is chargable upon its administration, and not upon its founders. The wit of man could not devise a national government that will go of itself. With an imbecile Executive, the strongest national government becomes imbecile.

It is not proposed, to present here, a plan of operations for our Government, much less, to enter into details. We are treating of principles — endeavoring to trace, to their logical consequences, conceded facts, and known political forces — human interests, prejudices, passions and ambitions. But we will suggest, in passing, that, in our judgment, it is not so material what particular position we shall first defend, as it is, that we immediately cease to acquiesce in rebellion, and defend, with a strong hand, and unfaltering determination, our national existence and rights.

Fortunately our system of government is such, that vindication of its national authority, does not require the overrunning of the States with armies. Most of the functions of government are, at all times, left to the States, to be there exercised, independently of the General Government. With these, the General Government has no occasion to concern itself directly, but only (when called on for the purpose) to maintain the rightful authority over them, of the State governments. With other national governments this is not so, and a rebellion arising, anywhere, under them, must be overcome in detail, as well as in general. But if the nature of our governmental system thus excuses us from the necessity of overrunning, with armies, the States where the authority of the General Government is denied, it does not excuse us, but, on the contrary, imposes, if possible, a stronger obligation on the General Government, to maintain its own few and simple, but most important rights, and to resist and punish their usurpation. And we are sure it will still be found, as, thus far in our history, it always has been found, that this division of duties between the State governments and the General Government, derogates not at all from the power and efficiency of the latter, but makes it, for its proper, constitutional, and general purposes, *the strongest and most efficient national government in the world.*

Suppose then, that our General Government, speaking and acting through the men who, clothed with its authority, have the right and duty to speak and act in its name, determines, as it seems at length to have done, that in no possible event, will it acquiesce in usurpation, and suffer its own dissolution to even begin ; but will, to the full extent of the nation's power, vindicate against enemies at home, as it cannot be doubted it would, against enemies abroad, its right and its duty to exist, to flourish unscathed, and to progress, as it has, and as the fathers meant it should, now and forever. And suppose it manifests such determination, by such immediate preparation as the exigencies of the case require,—taking special care, by the liberal use of its resources, to guard against any failure in the exercise of its power; and, if need be, that it exercise that power, unflinchingly and firmly. Can reasonable men doubt the result? Can it possibly be doubted that the final result will be, the maintenance of our Constitution — our Government —*as it is?* If there be such doubt in this case, then when, in the possible course of human events, can an occasion arrise, when the right can maintain itself, against the wrong?

But let us consider calmly the possible consequences. We will suppose, first, that the worst that has been threatened, should actually occur, and, that the Slave States, all of them, rush, at once, into civil war. How will the case stand, and how will it appear before the world, and in the thoughts of the people everywhere? The General Government, the government *de facto et de jure,* with its written constitution vindicating its course, is right in law and in morals, and has the universal sympathy of humanity, and the hearty approval of all nations. It has, too, immense superiority in numbers, in wealth, in ships, and in all the resources of war. Its opponents are destitute both of justification and of means, and can get no help. They will fight hopelessly *for slavery.* There can be but one possible result, — the right will certainly prevail, and the wrong be compelled to yield.

But "blood will flow and men will be killed!" True, but there are worse possible things than this ; to wit, national degradation, loss of liberty, submission to slavery.

> " Woe to the land thou tramplest o'er,
> Death-dealing Fiend of War ! "

But precisely because war is terrible, and peace most desirable, is it the solemn duty of this nation to defend itself against impending dissolution. He has read history with little profit, who does not know that the establishment of a filibustering slave-government, with national power, on the Gulf of Mexico is, in and of itself, a standing declaration of war; wars for our own curtailed and miserable national existence,—wars, too, in which European nations will ultimately participate,—wars, the final result of which no man is now wise enough to foretell, but in regard to which, every man should now be wise enough to know, that years of strife, thousands of lives, and millions of money, if necessary, expended now, in sustaining our present republican system, would be far the most economical and humane. We can think of no one advantage likely to result from a selfish and cowardly acquiescence now, in our national dissolution; for the difficulties and wars sure to follow, would come so soon, in these fast times, that very few of the fogies who would now compromise, would escape, through age, liability to military service, from which they are not already exempt. The trials and tribulations would not even be cast upon posterity.

Having contemplated the worst possible view, let us now consider one, more correspondent to probabilities.* Our government has shown itself exceedingly lenient, forbearing, peace-loving— not to say timid, vacillating, weak. The second officer in the new

* This was written previous to April 15 : events transpiring since, may cause it to seem less timely, but the principles remain, though the facts to which they are applied, be changed or modified.

" Confederacy," congratulating a large audience, lately, at Savannah, Georgia, on the successful progress of the revolution, said :

"I take this occasion to state that I was not without grave and serious apprehensions that, if the worst came to the worst, and cutting loose from the old government would be the only remedy for our safety and security, it would be attended with much more serious ills than it has been as yet."

Yet, forbearing, and even accommodating as our government has been, nevertheless, wherever and whenever it has been firm, slavery and its revolution have been stayed. It has attacked, where there was no resistance, and waited long, where the resistance was small. We think the inference reasonable, that, in view of such decisive determination and preparation by our government, as has been indicated, slavery and its revolution will, ere long, everywhere, pause; that peace, and not war, may be the result, and national salvation, not only, but the lives of the people, be secured. We think that slavery has not expected such action of our general government, and that this, more than anything else, has encouraged its attempted revolution.

The border Slave States, having the alternative, at once and distinctly, placed before them, will, we think, be less likely, to rush into a violent defence of the wrong and weak side, against the right and strong side, than they would be, to be drawn, by half-way measures, first into controversy, and then into false positions, and thus become committed to a course ending in hostilities.

We are aware that the balanced state of affairs was, in some respects, exceedingly favorable to the border Slave States, that it gave them great political importance, and that nothing could be more desirable to the managing politicians in those States, than its indefinite continuance; but such is not really the interest of the people of those States. To them, as to the people of all the States, it is far more important, that the state of doubtful anxiety should be terminated ; and we doubt not, that, in view of such determination and preparation by our government, could the question be fairly presented to the people of those States, they would, by overwhelming majorities, determine to maintain the government as it is, and refuse to engage in rebellion. Those States have been in the anamolous position of trying to do both. Pressed to the alternative, we think they will choose the former.

We have already explained, however, that, as a rule, in all the Slave States, slavery controls the State government, but checked, more or less, in the degree of its absolutism, by popular influences; that is, by republicanism. The controversy which has, perhaps, generally been supposed to refer to South and North, exists, in reality, in every Slave State, between republicanism and slavery; as much within the State lines of Virginia, as anywhere in our country. We think, also, that slavery understands this, dreads it, and that here, is its chief cause of anxiety; —that its greatest apprehensions, are from the people of its own States, from the spread and influence of republicanism, and the ultimate action of its own State governments, and not from any apprehended action of the general government; and we think, too, that the people of those States, the other party in the coming, though, perhaps, still distant contest there, are not so well aware, as slavery is, of the inherent antagonism between them and slavery. We therefore do not consider it certain, that slavery will not, in some, perhaps most, of the border Slave States, attempt, if circumstances should favor, to carry out its threat of "precipitating the revolution." Yet we know that slavery, however defiant and blustering, and apparently, reckless, is necessarily timid and cautious; and we therefore have strong hopes, that, in view of such determination and preparation by our government, (would that they had been earlier exhibited), slavery, in these States, will wisely determine to accept the continued sway of our government as it is, together with such lease of its own existence and power, as the several State governments and their people may choose to give.

A more dangerous element, in determining the course of these States, will be their ambitious politicians. These may be desperate enough for the plunge; for they have been nursed into factitious importance. But politicians, too, are timid — very timid, and our government is strong—very strong, and its friendship better, even for a politician, than its hostility.

Public opinion, the common sense of the people, may have a preponderating influence in these States; and its influence will be greater, the naked question—support of our government, or rebellion? — being at once presented, and without alternative, than if it were farther complicated by political manoeuverings and delay.

Such we think a rational view of probabilities. But we desire, here, to insist, that, for nations, as for individuals, it is not well to determine our course exclusively by reference to consequences, or—what is all that we can get in that direction—by our *estimate* of consequences. Man's estimate of consequences is unreliable at the best; but an all-wise Providence rules the world, and where the right lies plain before us, as we think, in this case, it does, it would be assuming too large a risk, to attempt to compromise it, in order to accommodate our views of consequences. "Do right though the heavens fall," is a good rule, not because the heavens fall thereby, but because they do not,—because the God-established relation between right action and good results, is found, by practical experience, to be safer as a guide, than man's judgment of consequences. We believe that an infidel apprehension of danger to result from the doing of political duty, has brought us into our greatest national danger, and that, an immediate and trustful performance of that duty, will do most to extricate us.

Looking calmly at the greatest dangers foretold by the timid, looking rationally at probabilities, or looking simply at the duties plainly before us in the way of administering our government according to its constitution and laws, we can arrive at but one conclusion, satisfactory to reason, or at all becoming a great, wise, free, God-fearing, and man-loving people, or accordant with our past history, or with our professed confidence in the government of our choice; and that is, for our government to go strongly and confidently forward, as it has for seventy years, leaving those who may attempt to oppose it, whoever or wherever they may be, to go down before a necessity of the age, infinitely greater and stronger than any which they can pretend to represent.

The duty of this people and of this nation in this crisis, cannot innocently be evaded. Considerations of immediate pecuniary thrift, desire for peace at any price, an overmastering horror of blood-shed, are no excuse for national dereliction; and certainly our position in the world, and in the world's history, will afford us no peculiar exemption now, but, on the contrary, they require us, by every consideration that can be addressed to a great nation, and to reasonable and brave men, to act, confidently and fearlessly, the part assigned us. The American revolution was the beginning of a political system, the conduct of which is now in our hands, and its great and ultimate purposes are still unaccomplished. How great and excellent a system it is, and also how it is fitted and expected to secure the public safety and happiness, are well shown in the clear language of Mr. Calhoun, quoted near the beginning of this essay. Republicanism in every State, the rational control, by the people, of their political affairs, undisturbed by force or violence, with full sway for all moral influences, guaranteed by the general government, is the system which our fathers established, which the world has admired, and we have so long used and enjoyed, and of which, even Mr. Calhoun declared, "the Federal Constitution and Government will stand, more durable than brass, an everlasting monument of their wisdom and patriotism."

We have shown that this republican system is not in practical operation in the Slave States, that another system, hostile to republicanism, has usurped the political power in those States, that, aware of the antagonism between itself and our republican system, it has determined to seek its own preservation at the expense of a revolution that shall destroy our republican system. Performance of the duty which we have pointed out, of resisting this aggression promptly and with strong hands, if need be, to the utmost of our national power and resources, prepares the way for the restoration of republicanism in every State in the Union; thus securing the harmony of our system, and complying with a fundamental provision of our Constitution.

Slavery, as it existed in the States at the formation of our Constitution, is not to be attacked by our general government, however great may be the provocation; but slavery, organizing as a national power, and advancing to the overthrow of republicanism, and the destruction of our government, must be resisted and attacked, without hesitation and without compromise, by the government which it would destroy. To say that it cannot live under our Constitution as it is, to say that it is in danger of extinction from the advancing power and influence of republicanism in the States, is no justification for its rebellion. It has no right to live a single moment, in any State in the Union, longer than it can live there, with republicanism. Ours is a republican Union and Constitution; not a slavery Union and Constitution. Republicanism is guaranteed in every State; slavery is not guaranteed in a single State; and no administration of our general government can, without becoming forsworn, forego its duty to preserve our republican system in every State. If, therefore, slavery is right, when it alleges that it cannot safely live under our republican system of government—under our Constitution as it is, and in the same States with republicanism, then the time has come for it to prepare, becomingly, for its dissolution; for republicanism must, certainly, live, and not die.

Suppose that this be, in reality, the case—and we have already more than intimated our belief that it is—it strengthens, rather than weakens, the solemn obligations resting on our government and its administration, to maintain our system now, and to resist revolution, to the utmost of our national power. If slavery, in the Slave States, begins to feel the reins of power slipping in its palsied hands, how disastrous it would be for the republican people of those States, numbers of whom have watched, and waited, and struggled long, if, through the pusillanimity of our general government, slavery should be permitted to extort a new lease of power, by forcing on a revolution for this express purpose!

If, as we have all learned, undoubtingly to believe, republicanism be the best form of government for man, and our federative system the best practical form of republicanism, what precious hopes of the people, in the Slave States, and of the people who shall hereafter be in those States, in all time, what hopes, too, of the good and the free, everywhere,—aye, and of the oppressed, everywhere, depend, now, on the performance, by our general government, of its simple, constitutional duty; the duty of self-preservation, and therein, the constitutional duty of guaranteeing republicanism in every State!

The revival of republicanism in the Slave States, will naturally, perhaps necessarily, follow the defeat of the revolution prepared and urged on by slavery; and then, in those States, gag-law and Lynch-law, will give way to common-law, and statute-law, and vigilance committees be superceded by civil authorities. In the language of Mr. Calhoun:—" Violence and revolution or physical force, as the means of change," will be " excluded " there, and the " doors " opened —" never again to be closed — for the free and full operation of all the moral elements in favor of change," " The liberty of the press — the freedom of speech and

3

debate — the trial by jury — the privilege of *habeas corpus* — and the right of the people peaceably to assemble together and petition for a redress of grievances," "put under the sacred guarantee of the Federal Constitution, and secured to the citizens against the power, both of the Federal and State governments," will become real and practical — "if the Federal Government shall do its duty under the guarantees of the Constitution, by thus promptly suppressing physical force as an element of change."

Republicanism in the Free States also depends, probably, on the preservation of our national system. Our great, strong nation, has proved to be — what it was intended — a perfect wall of defence, an overshadowing providence, for the exceedingly free and popular republicanism of the several States. It cannot possibly be so in the future, certainly not to the extent it has been, if this great, strong Government shall now dissolve "like the baseless fabric of a vision."

Permit the revolution which slavery has initiated, which it certainly intends, and will, as certainly accomplish, unless it shall encounter a superior force, whether in five States or fifteen, and the power and prestige of the American Republic, are fatally destroyed. The wise national measures of all our statesmen, as well of those who founded our government as of those who have enlarged and strengthened it, are, at once, rendered nugatory. The mouth of the Mississippi, the southern coast, our vast Pacific territory, and, perhaps, other important integral parts of our country, are lost to us; and commercial restrictions and national dangers gather in upon us, with the rapidly contracting national size and strength, involving, most undoubtedly, in the near future, the goading necessity of using far greater force, to preserve even life, and a modicum of liberty, than will now be required to preserve the whole.

But, say, with the authority of this great nation, to slavery and its revolution, "thus far — no farther," and republicanism, renewed in its youth, smiles again, serene and secure, in every State. Slavery, yielding to a greater necessity, not only abandons its aspirations for distinct national embodiment, but retires from the field of our national politics, and shields itself, as it may, and as it was contented to do, previous to 1840, under the legislation of States, that are themselves protected from violence from without and from within, by the great and strong government, which slavery, in its arrogance, has aspired to overthrow. There, and there only, can the problem which it presents, find a peaceful solution. What that solution may be, we will not assume to declare, but, that thus this problem may be solved, peacefully solved, our faith in man, and our trust in a Higher Power, will not permit us to doubt.

In the meantime, our nation, released from its only internal danger, and exempt, as it long has been, from external dangers, may continue, with fresh impulse, its grand and happy career. It is a narrow view that limits our republican system to its present boundaries. We think it a narrow view, to limit it to North America — perhaps it is too narrow, to limit it to the continent. The advantages resulting from perfect freedom of intercourse between the people of the several States, are such as cannot be secured under diverse national governments. One great source of our unexampled national prosperity, is in our exemption, among so many States, and of so varied climates and productions, from every kind and degree of governmental espionage and obstruction, in our exchanges of the fruits of our soil and industry. But the moral benefits thence resulting, are still greater, and altogether incalculable. It was not by an accident, that, in former language, *stranger* meant *enemy*. Mutual interests, and mutual knowledge of one another, make friends of men, and the national government that protects and encourages such mutual intercourse, becomes the recognized benefactor of all.

Governmental science, taught by examples in the several States, is also making, under our system, wonderful progress, and is, in turn, both teaching and exemplifying the absurdity of the old dogma, that man is naturally the enemy of man, and is substituting for it, the christian doctrine, "behold, all ye are brethren." Under such a system it is no unnatural development — however strange it may be, in the world's history — the national charity that fed the famishing poor in Ireland, that springs to the aid of suffering Kansas, and that even now, hastens to supply the hungry demands of the people, in Alabama and Mississippi. Such things are the natural results of our republican system, a system more in accordance, than any that the world has before seen, with the songs of the angels, who declared "peace on earth, and good will to men!"

And the improvements and discoveries of the age, those especi-

ally relating to transportation for goods, for persons, and for
thoughts — steamships, railroads, printing-presses, telegraphs —
seem to be specially adapted to the expanding needs and capabil-
ities of our grand republican system. Other governments might
well dread the dangers of territorial expansion. With their sys
tems, and with their means of conducting them, national ambition frequently outran their national ability. To the harmonious
and efficient action of our system, national expansion scarcely
seems to place, in these times, any assignable limits. To the
exercise of the few, but most important functions of our General
Government, space and distance scarcely present obstructions.

Won by the observed harmony, large practical freedom, and
perfect safety of the States in our system, other States will press
into the charmed circle : and, not by unwilling conquest, but by
mutual beneficial arrangement, and as fast as development and
adaptation permit, the regions north of us, to the Pole, and south
of us, to the Isthmus, and even the rich Savannahs watered by
the Amazon and the La Plata, may gladly and happily congre-
gate, by their representatives at Washington, and derive, from the
government founded by our fathers, assured protection, peace,
and republican liberty and independence. Thus we have, on this
continent, " a congress of nations" for the peaceful adjustment of
national questions.

The genius of our people, extending with our institutions, will
spread our improvements over the continent ; and all will participate in the benefits. Varieties of climate will minister, as they
ought, to the people's health, wealth and happiness. Fresh fruits
in every season, will be everywhere easily obtained. The tropics
will be the hot-houses of the market gardens, for our northern
cities, villages and towns ; and productions in the higher latitudes,
so abundant as to be seemingly useless, will minister gratefully to
the languid dwellers nearer the equator.

As our national power rises, expands and grows, enterprises,
now seeming absurdly impracticable, or requiring the combined
energies of great nations, will become easily practicable for our
own. Pacific railroads,—not one or two, but all that our millions
of people will require and sustain — will dart over the continent
wherever needed, and with as much seeming ease, as the spider
throws out its web on the breeze. A ship-canal across the Isthmus, — not meandering circuitously through valleys, and rising,
by means of locks, over a summit level, but broad, level and

straight, under the ridge, from ocean to ocean will transport the commerce of the world. With such facilities, Oregon and California, Chili and Peru, will be nearer to our political and commercial centers, Washington and New-York, practically, and measuring by time, than was New-Orleans during the administration of Jefferson.

These, and perhaps still greater, and, as yet, unthought of enterprises, successfully accomplished, will attest our national power, and add to our national glory. Yet, *not, if our National Government permits the revolution to go on, which slavery has begun;* not, if it does not immediately and effectively use its national power, for national protection, and for a lasting warning to all, that no real success can attend here, violence, anarchy and rebellion. Using again the language of Mr. Calhoun, we say : " No people ever had so fair a start. All that is lacking is, that we shall understand, in all its great and beautiful proportions, the noble political structure reared by the wisdom and patriotism of our ancestors, and to have the virtue and the sense to preserve and protect it."

Certain supposed obstacles deserve, perhaps, a passing notice. It is said that the States which have "seceded" will never humble themselves by submission. We have failed entirely, in one of our chief purposes, if it does not sufficiently appear, that it is not properly the republican States of this Union that have engaged in revolution, but a power in antagonism to the republican people of those States, that has usurped political control, and wrongfully assumes now, to speak in the name of the people and of the States. Every indication is given by this power, that it is consciously a usurper. Precipitation, terror, violence, and not the sober second thought of the people, are what it relies on. The restoration of republican independence to these people and States, under the guarantees of the Constitution, and by the power of the Union, will not come to them in the shape of tyrannical subjugation, but in the shape, rather, of real enfranchisement.

In several of these States it is already known that a majority of the people, not only have not desired, but are actually opposed to the revolution forced on them by the usurping power. And it cannot be doubted that, in every State, with proper time for reflection, and fair opportunity for the action of those "great moral agents," spoken of by Mr. Calhoun, the people would hold, with gladness, in the Union, to their guaranteed safety, freedom and republicanism.

The men who now lead on the revolution in those States, will, it is true, be compelled to give way. But their humiliation involves no humiliation for their States. Other men in those States, good and true, will be found by their people, competent to lead in the wiser, safer and happier paths of union and peace. Moreover, people easily forgive themselves, even when they have erred.

Certain it is, that, in every State, are great numbers of men, faithful to truth, duty and constitutional obligations; and not even an accidental majority against them, in their own States respectively, can absolve our General Government from the sacred duty it owes, to sustain and vindicate them; not indeed, by placing the State Governments in their hands, but by protecting their rights as minorities, in States in the Union. If the purpose of Constitutions be, as Mr. Calhoun says, to restrain majorities, certainly our United States Constitution should now avail for the political salvation of our loyal people in every State. Impotent as these people are, in many of the Slave States, if unaided, yet, sustained by the general government, they may, by use of "the moral agencies" guaranteed to them by the Constitution, restore to legitimate action, in their States, the republican principles of our system.

We have purposely avoided, as much as possible, in this exposition, the use of names, especially of living political men; and gladly would we close, without reference to the political manipulators and their combinations, throughout the Union. Really they ought not to influence the opinions or actions of any body, in times like these. But, being the cause, both of unfounded hopes and of unfounded fears, we notice them, to protest against their mischievous imbecility. Earnest men are for earnest times, — men who believe in duty and in God, not men who believe in sham and the devil. Political parties, that survive revolutionary times, are not those whose chief end and aim it is, to nurse themselves. The party that survives, is the one that finds the most useful work to do. In a crisis like this, when the fate of a continent seems trembling in the balance, the petty interests and ambitions of the petty men who flutter and buzz in the sunny day of prosperity, should not be permitted to usurp public attention.

Plans for the construction or reconstruction of parties, are useless, and will be destitute of power to harm those who go boldly forward in the performance of the duties which patriotism, the Constitution and the laws enjoin.

But woe to the men, conspicuous or obscure, who oppose, or shrink, or equivocate, now ! Nothing can be more certain, nothing is more in accordance with human nature, nothing is more in accordance with our past political history, than that the men who now sustain our republican government, wherever they may have been, or whatever called, heretofore, will be recognized, hereafter, as safe political guides, and safe depositories of political power; and that the men who now connive, in any manner whatever, at rebellion, or who hesitate or compromise, wherever they may now stand, or whatever honored name they may now wear, will never outgrow their disgrace. Year by year, as the nation recedes from this time of its peril, clearer and clearer will become the universal consciousness of the broad distinction between the right and the wrong, as now presented before us ; and few, in the rising generation will, in a few years, have the charity to believe, that any who now take the wrong side, can possibly be good men.

April 15, 1861.

THE CRISIS: ITS RATIONALE.

PART II.—RESTORATION OF LEGITIMATE AUTHORITY THE END AND OBJECT OF THE WAR.

A year has passed since the foregoing pages were published. The public mind, then much tossed by conflicting counsels, needed clear ideas of the principles at work in the contest that was beginning—an understanding of the rationale of the crisis. Its magnitude and earnest reality were comprehended by few; the leaders of public action differed widely; consequently, a great and intelligent nation stood paralyzed with doubt, and only those banded for rebellion seemed inspired and sustained by a definite purpose. It was time for action rather than for explanation; yet the great hindrance to effective action was the want of clear notions of the work to be done. Errors of opinion erected themselves into real obstacles; and plainly now does it appear that, in every stage of this crisis, our nation has been punished for these errors, too long unadvisedly or selfishly entertained.

Clearer ideas of political duty now prevail, and the true men of the nation are more united by definite purpose. This is not merely because events have more and more lifted the veil, but it is also because *they have compelled the people to think.* The people of a republic must think, or they must fail. Earnest thought, inspiring earnest action, has done much to bear us through this crisis; yet the future is still before us. This is a great republic, it is *the* great republic, and it is ours—yours, reader, and mine. This trial of our reign is not yet fully past. Perhaps the most difficult—we hope not the most dangerous—part is yet before us. Not for speculation, therefore, but for present and important use, let us consider further the rationale of this great crisis in our national life.

Time has already done much to verify the principles, and, in fact, every material proposition in the foregoing exposition; in so much that a review and comparison with subsequent and actual

3*

events, though made for the purpose of establishing conviction, would be liable to a different construction. Such review and comparison are left for the reader to make, with the reminder that whatever of accuracy may thus appear, in what was written almost entirely before the attack on Fort Sumter, is attributable neither to prophetic gifts nor to lucky guessing, but simply to logical inferences from well-known political principles.

What shall follow is not intended as a repetition or mere enforcement of what precedes; yet, being part of the same great subject, and intimately connected, the principles already established should be borne in mind. Thoughtful consideration may lead, not only to the formation of better opinions and the dismissal of needless apprehensions, but also to wiser and more effective action.

Accepting the admission which invariably connects slavery with the contest in which the country is engaged, we exposed, in the foregoing pages, the fallacy which treats slavery as geographical and subject to the laws of political economy prevailing in free communities, and which assumes that it will die of its own accord; and showed how the anti-republican system which it necessitates in every Slave State, prevents the interests of the masses from working its abolishment through republicanism, anywhere, so long as the slave interest dominates the State; that the principles of slavery being inherent and characteristic, and ministering everywhere to the cupidity of the master, though ruinous to the State, are independent of climate and productions; consequently, that the interest of the master, the pecuniary value of which is everywhere fairly measured by the price of slaves, will, in no climate or country, cause slaveholders to abolish or discourage slavery, or to establish or permit active republicanism.

A kindred fallacy is that with which the people of this country have too long deluded themselves, namely : that our slavery is only African or negro slavery, and therefore less dangerous or more tolerable.

Every vice or wickedness, public or private, seeks justification or palliation under the cover of some exception. Suppose the negro be inferior, he is nevertheless a man, and endowed by his Creator with the rights of a man. Assumed inferiority, its corelative of course being superiority, is the ground of all anti-republican governments and pretensions. Let republicans beware of sophistries which undermine the foundations of their own liberty. Ethnological distinctions afford no tenable ground for the denial of human rights. Association, honors, offices, are voluntary in free communities, and do not necessarily follow the acknowledgment of rights; yet the fallacy that they do necessarily follow is constantly adduced to sustain the denial of rights to those whom we may suppose it is our interest to wrong.

We may not desire, and it may not be wise policy, to elevate to the presidency, or to the office of justice of the peace, or to marry, an African, a Malay, a Hindoo, a Chinese, a Turk, or an Egyptian; and doubtless many among us would extend the same exclusion to most or all Asiatic, European, African, and South American races; but all of these races, or, in short, every *man* has a God-derived right to his liberty — to his wife, to his children, to the fruits of his own labor, and to a fair opportunity, unobstructed by other men, for the cultivation and improvement of his own mental and moral powers, such as they may be.

But, completely as the ethnological argument fails, on examination, to justify *our* slavery, it is also becoming more and more inapplicable. Where the control of white men is absolute, and the condition of the offspring follows that of the mother, as it does universally in the Slave States, the ethnological character of slaves must change; not rapidly, perhaps, during the life of an individual, but with great and accelerated rapidity, during the life of a nation. Observation confirms what reason suggests.

In 1850 the State of Kentucky contained 32,359 mulattoes, and the State of Virginia 79,775; there were, in all the Slave States, 348,874.*

In the course of a few generations the proportion of African blood in these becomes very small, yet the *status* continues. Ethnology does not save the blood of even the "superior race" from bondage.

The Richmond *Inquirer*, in December, 1855, said:

"The laws of all the southern States justify the holding of white men in slavery, provided, through the mother they are descended, however remotely, from a negro slave." "— the principle of slavery is right, and does not depend on difference of complexion."

* See, also, "Sea Board Slave States," p. 594, etc., on mixed races at New Orleans.

If the presumed inferiority of the negro were the real reason for *our* slavery, then slavery should cease when the negro blood gives place to the boasted Anglo-Saxon. It does not cease in such cases; but, on the contrary, becomes more valuable for the purposes of bondage, and is held to with greater tenacity. Slaveholders themselves no longer claim to justify mere negro slavery, but insist that slavery is the proper and normal condition of the laboring class, everywhere, whatever their origin or complexion. And persons not slaveholders, even persons of standing and political influence in the free States, have lent to the doctrine at least a negative acquiescence — sometimes even more. A representative man of the late dominant party, reared, petted and advanced by the free States, was conspicuous for having, throughout a protracted political career, carefully abstained from commendation of liberty as a principle; and he even took pains to declare, in the Senate, that he cared not whether slavery was voted up or voted down; and the declaration was made, not for the purpose of signalizing any peculiar or personal opinions, but, on the contrary, to manifest his conservative moderation.

A writer, also, in the North American Review did not hesitate to say, in 1853:

"Slavery, therefore, exists rightfully in the South. No rights of the negro are violated when he is made a slave. His right, like that of all men, is to be governed for his own benefit. Some even go so far as to maintain that a social relation, founded on the same principles, and modified to suit different circumstances, a relation more strict than that of master and apprentice, and less severe and permanent than that of slavery, might, with equal justice and much advantage, be introduced into some of the northern States in relation, not only to negroes, but to the swarms of emigrants who crowd our shores, many of them equally degraded by ignorance, poverty and vice, and equally needing care, guidance and government. Less liberty in them and more authority over them would be alike beneficial to themselves and society."

Selfish cupidity is the real cause and motive for slavery wherever it exists, and occasionally the admission is made with sufficient plainness to be understood.

A leading southern paper alleged, five years ago:

"It is not hatred of slavery, it is not sympathy for the negro, which kindles the resentment and enthusiasm of the black republican party. It is envy of the ease and affluence of the southern gentlemen and jealousy of the aristocratic character of our social system which constitute the sentiment of abolitionism."

This allegation of motives reveals motives as plainly, perhaps, as the language lately quoted by a western correspondent of a Boston paper:

"This lady," says he, "coming from the north, loves slavery for this reason, given in her own words : 'O, the slaveholders are so independent and live so easy ! They can get rich in a few years, and there is no class in the world that can enjoy more than they.'"

This brings us back to the old foundations. *Our* slavery rests on the same bad and selfish principles on which slavery has always rested ; the same principles, in fact, which have given their support to aristocracy, to monarchy, and to every form of tyranny and despotism. That which divides us now is no abstract opinion about races, but it is *slavery*, the oldest, the greatest, the worst, and the most dreaded political enemy of the human race. The issue between us is simply one of principle, applying to man, rather than to a particular class of men ; and it reaches to the very form and nature of government.

What is slavery ? It is negation of self-control. It is the compulsory subjection of the faculties and powers of one human being to the control of another human being. It is necessarily social in its character, and pertains to order and to government ; but it is the lowest possible form of social order and government. The restraint to which it subjects a human being is ultimate in its degradation. It is not that to which a child or a lunatic is subjected, when reason is wanting, for in such case the good of the subject is the leading idea ; but it is that to which we subject an animal. It is negation of the use of reason and of self-direction. It is the appropriation of another's energies without reciprocity, the master's interest and will being the sole measure and guide. Its motive is cupidity, its argument force. In government it is most simple, and it is most absolute. Other modes of government have, or, at least, appear to have, reference to mutual benefits. The government of slavery is entirely one-sided. Its order, its regulations, its practices, originate and exist entirely in the master's interest and convenience. Even those which relate to the slave's comfort or enjoyment are measured and limited by the master's interest. Cupidity is the supreme arbiter on one side, entire submission the all-comprehensive duty on the other.

The republicanism of this country is democratic, not aristo-

cratic. Its fundamental principle is human rights — the rights of
all, and not the rights of any special class as against others ; much
less is it privilege. Sovereignty is of the people, and no man may
rightfully claim what he will not also concede. It is impossible
to conceive of any thing more irreconcilable than slavery and republicanism — such republicanism as we profess. Every principle of the one is abhorrent to every principle of the other. They
can not permanently coëxist in the same country and under the
same government. They could only coëxist while slavery was
regarded as an exception and in the process and preparation for
removal. This is not matter of opinion, but of demonstration ;
for, as the philosopher eliminates with confidence all the elements
of great and abstruse problems from given data, so may we with
certainty infer, from the principles of our republican system, the
incompatibility of slavery, and hence its ultimate extinction. Our
fathers expected and meant it should pass away from among us.
We know this, not only from what they said, but from the essential and inherent nature of the system they established.

This is so, not only in its nature, and as our fathers saw it and
intended to have it, but it is perfectly obvious, also, to the conductors of this rebellion, more obvious, perhaps, to them, even,
than to ourselves. The most of us have assumed the continuance
and preservation of republican principles as matters of course,
and have trusted too much, perhaps, to their unaided operation.
Not so, however, with slaveholders and the political slave interest. They, not less than the founders of our government, understand the operation of causes and the logical sequence of effects,
and with intellects sharpened by interest, they realize that slavery
and republicanism are irreconcilable. Whenever, therefore, they
resolved *to hold on to slavery*, they became, by inexorable logic,
*necessarily hostile to republicanism and to our republican system
of government*. They who could not or would not see this, have
sometimes called them mad ; but patient observers of facts and
principles must admit that their madness has a method in it, and
consists only in believing, or at least determining, that slavery
must be sustained. Grant this, and all else which they claim and
do becomes reasonable and proper. It is precisely what any people should claim and do, if reasonable and consistent, in order to
sustain the same principle.

It was nothing special done by the believers in republicanism that alarmed the believers in slavery, and rendered them hostile. Pretexts subserved a purpose; but the cause was the inherent nature and principles of republicanism and their embodiment and expression in our system of government — free schools, free speech, general suffrage, and social equality.

The Charleston *Mercury*, in the spring of 1856, argued and showed, in a series of carefully prepared articles, that, whenever two hostile forms of civilization are associated in political union, one of them must inevitably be absorbed by the other, and that, under the Federal Constitution, the South must eventually be swallowed up by "the North" — meaning, thereby, republicanism. It said:

"If there be any phenomenon, which may be more clearly understood than any other which is presented by the development of civil society in the United States, it is this: that *the social system and civilization of the North and the northern method of thought*, completely Europeanized as it is, *will predominate in the American Union, if that Union lasts;* and Federal Government yielding to the pressure of that social system and method of thought, will, by the action of the representative body upon it, become, and in a great degree is now, merely the agent and instrument by which that predominance is to be accomplished. That the South is even now undergoing the process of absorption by the northern method of thought, in the manner stated by the above postulate or law, needs but a common sense observation to determine."

This writer fully appreciated the necessities of the republican system, and denouncing, as traitors to the rights and interests of the South, those southern representatives who then consented to act in harmony with the North with a view to controlling the whole, he said:

"So far from the idea being true, upon which southern statesmanship founds its hopes, if the Federal Government were blotted out at a single blow, the method of northern thought would not be changed, the social system of the North would progress as before, and a political system born of the joint action of both would be formed and controlled by them, to the subservience of all the ends they seek to accomplish now by means of the Federal Government. But a good would result to the South by the fall of that government, for the present Union would be formed no more, and the South would thus cease to be under the blight and curse of a southern representation to a northern congress."

An intelligent correspondent of the same paper, writing from Washington, January 11, 1857, says:

"We can not hope for any other solution of this anti-slavery problem than the ultimate triumph of free soil over every department of government. All efforts at resistance will be as idle in the future as in the past.

There are occasions in the history of nations, as well as of individuals, when extraordinary efforts are necessary to resist the effect of causes which may seem indirect, or even immaterial to the world at large. The slave owners of the South find themselves surrounded by elements which must end in their utter destruction, unless some great, determined and concerted effort is made in resistance."   *   *   *   "Every effort of the South to escape from the thraldom will be deemed revolutionary. It is the first and highest duty of the South to prepare to meet the issue thus presented to us boldly. South Carolina will be sustained if she accepts the conflict. To do so successfully, she must establish a policy looking to eventual independence. All the mere political expedients or party appliances will come to nought. The press of the State should combine to develop that organization of individual sentiment which is necessary to practical effort."

Understanding so well and so correctly the incompatibility of republicanism with slavery, seeing and knowing that the difference is radical and fundamental, yet, *determined in every event to hold on to slavery*, what could the slaveholders and the political slave interest so rationally do, as deliberately, carefully, but determinedly, to revolt from a republican government? Under such circumstances, the thing itself had of course to be done, or at least attempted; the remaining question being obviously only one of time and opportunity. And if it had to be done, or attempted, how could reasoning men be expected to forego the use of an occasion so peculiarly favorable as was afforded them by a series of remarkably acquiescent administrations of our general government — a series, too, that was evidently approaching its close? The real wonder is, not that they availed themselves of the opportunity, but that it was so wonderfully prepared and offered to them. Not madly, and not foolishly, has the occasion been either chosen or used. The leaders of the rebellion have committed but one essential error. It consists simply *in clinging to slavery* — in saying to evil : "be thou my good."

We would add that, on the question of expediency, they erred also in supposing that in this age and in this country, a rebellion against republicanism, for the express purpose of establishing a government for slavery, could succeed ; but, witnessing the ready sympathy extended to them by rival governments anxious to attend the obsequies of republicanism, knowing, too, how many there are among ourselves who have learned to think that the slave interest must succeed in whatever it really undertakes, and who probably are still ready and willing to seek its favor, and understanding how self-confident men become who are self-assertive, we are constrained to admit that, from their point of view, their scheme was far from appearing absurdly impracticable.

The great moral principle which lies at the foundation of this whole subject must not be overlooked. Slavery is *wrong ;* and the light which enlightens every man coming into the world enables all to know it. The force of the truth embodied in the golden rule is acknowledged, or at least in some degree felt, by every human being ; and no perversity of educational influences, or repetition of sophistries, can completely blind any one to the inherent moral wrong of slavery ; much less can a whole people blind themselves to this truth. Slaveholders know that slavery is wrong, however they may pettifog with their consciences on the subject, and use their interests as counselors. But the responsibility for seeking to pervert judgment concerning it rests not with slaveholders only. Too long have our whole people been paltering with this subject, inventing euphemisms for it, and forgetting, in their selfishness, that God is just, and that *righteousness* — not *wrong* — exalteth a nation.

The question, between the two sides in this case, refers to first principles. If slavery is right, then the rebellion is right; because it is necessary for the perpetuation of slavery. If slavery is wrong, then its supporters are wrong ; and have no right to rebel against republicanism and its government; but they who defend them are right, and engaged in the cause of humanity and of God.

It may be suggested that each side may think itself right. But it is not so. Moral distinctions are too plain for such confusion. On questions for the intellect, and even on questions of fact, there is much room for honest differences of opinion; but on moral questions it is different ; and on questions so simple as that of slavery, the test is too easily applied to leave reasonable grounds for a plea of ignorance, especially in this age and country. Moreover, the right and the wrong on this subject have long ago been settled by the united testimony of the great and good of every age and clime. We say, unhesitatingly, therefore, that they who are engaged in this rebellion know instinctively that their cause is bad, and that the enlightened moral opinion of the world is against them.

Hence their implacable hatred. Men determined to hold to a great wrong, and to defend it with strong hand, find it necessary to cultivate in every possible way all the savageness of their natures, are compelled to steel themselves against the promptings of humanity and to cultivate bitter hatred against those who oppose

4 ·

them. Were they to yield to the influences of brotherly kindness, their cause itself must immediately fail.

Slavery can not meet republicanism on equal ground, but must answer with passion what it cannot answer with logic, and must make up for inherent weakness by remorseless violence. Consciously an aggressor and consciously in the wrong, it naturally hates those it injures. This has been so from the beginning, and the exhibitions of its hatred now witnessed with surprise, as causeless, are but the results of its natural development. Its hatred extends to all who do not acknowledge it to be right, and coöperate zealously and constantly to sustain it. It will not, because it safely can not, recognize degrees of approval. The history of all political men who, having begun to favor it, have anywhere hesitated or faltered, abundantly illustrates this. The monitor within and the evident sentiments of mankind compel it to know that only interest, constant and strong personal interest, is to be trusted in its cause. Hence the efforts of many among us to conciliate its quick sense of hostility, by joining in denunciation of its more open opponents, find their fit illustration in the labors of Sisyphus rolling the stone.

Were it possible really to believe slavery just, its champions, relying on that inherent justice, would be more tolerant. Were they consciously right, they might, even though unsuccessful, conduct war with magnanimity. As it is, they can only be boastfully "chivalrous," cruel and remorseless. The unities of the drama in which they are engaged imperatively require them to be so. It is most natural, therefore, that the war should be begun and conducted, on their part, with treachery, and should be attended by frequent exhibitions of malignity — that soldiers should be poisoned, the dead mutilated, graves desecrated, human bones used for trophies, and unarmed union men shot and hung.

That the vindictive malignity of those engaged in the rebellion is due to their principles, and not to mere sectional hostility, is shown by their treatment of people of their own States. A late number of the Richmond *Examiner*, speaking of union men in Virginia, says:

"The most of them have packed up, ready to leave for Yankeedom at the shortest possible notice. In Braxton county every tory has been shot by his neighbor, and in several other counties the citizens devoted to the confederate cause are doing good service in the same manner."

That cause is undoubtedly *the* cause of the bitterness which they exhibit, and in this fact appears the utter hopelessness of winning them to reconciliation by the exhibition of mere kindness. They know what republicanism requires of its friends, as well as what slavery requires of themselves; and, therefore, even acquiescence by the former in all the wishes and demands of the latter would bring no real love or respect, but rather contempt. Too far, already, has such acquiescence been carried, for the peace and happiness of all.

Were it the sole object of this people to open the way for mutual kindness, there is no means so direct or effective as to put down the rebellion of slavery with strong hand and in the least possible time. The friends of republicanism must act as though they believed in it and loved it. The hated and despised must become feared and respected, before they can be loved.

The necessities of slavery impose its character upon every part of this rebellion. It has been shown in the former part of this exposition that the social necessities of slavery require for it an anti-republican system, opposed to free speech, free thought and free action, and embodying the master's interest and will as the absolute law, in States dominated by the slave interest, even though organized under the forms of republicanism. What those same necessities would inevitably require in a government expressly formed for their accommodation, is not difficult to foresee. The world has seldom witnessed so effective and systematized degradation of the mass of human beings under a government, as such a system would infallibly produce. Men, it is true, are not always consistent; but facts, principles and history are terribly logical.

The London *Times*, ten years ago, made this correct statement of the principles on which the English Government is organized and conducted:

"The institutions and customs of this country are all adapted to the supposition of a vast difference of classes, — a lower class, redundant, necessitous, ignorant and manageable; an upper class, wealthy, exclusive, united and powerful; and a middle class, struggling to emerge from the lower and attach itself to the upper."

We see what moderate degree of general elevation such a system allows; but what could be hoped for humanity under a system in which the upper class would be wealthy, exclusive, united and powerful, with *two* lower classes, redundant, necessitons, ignorant and manageable, but *with no middle or transitionary class!* Schools can not aid the poor whites to rise; for education, except of the masters, is dangerous in a land of slaves, and therefore must be discouraged, and even forbidden. There is no hope for them, except to become the armed watch-dogs for slavery. The only accessions to the upper class are immigrating fortune-seekers. The result, embodied in a national government, would, inevitably, be the *ne plus ultra* of aristocratic selfishness and despotism.

Against the principles and system thus threatening to establish themselves here, are necessarily arrayed, in deadly hostility, our national principles and system. Republicanism, liberty, and all that our fathers meant, when they declared themselves contending for *the rights of man*, are now at stake. We are defending the system of government founded by our fathers, and which, for more than seventy years has, in every respect, save one, proved a miracle of success. We have deviated from its principles in administration, and hence, one of its normal results, the abolition of slavery, has been delayed, until slavery, instead of preparing for its dissolution, strengthens itself against the government and threatens its overthrow. Democratic republicanism is the essential principle embodied in our governmental system, and this, we have shown, is hostile to slavery. Slavery is aware of it — hence, the rebellion. Slavery is wise, but slavery is wrong. Our government — and with it republicanism, which is its soul — must be sustained.

Errors and obstructions have occurred in the administration of our government and in the political history of our people, which have caused many to misjudge as to the principles involved in this contest. An understanding of these errors and obstructions will make the true principles, and consequently our present duties, clearer now.

Erroneously, an idea has prevailed that our constitutional system sustains slavery; and logically, the idea has been developed and wrought, until numbers among us transfer to slavery the reverence due to the Constitution. With a considerable class even the word "constitution" seems to mean slavery; and hence, with them, to obey the Constitution is to sustain slavery. Whence this idea?

It originated in a perversion of a single provision of our Constitution, which, being unjustifiably made the subject of congressional legislation, has, like an unyielding foreign substance introduced into harmonious machinery, nearly caused the whole operations of our system to become jammed. Leading northern politicians in two great parties deemed it policy to sanction the legislation, and set themselves with industry to the task of reconciling an unwilling people to propositions instinctively revolting. What could not be done by logic, was attempted by iteration. Partizan feelings and vulgar prejudice helped the attempt. But, worst of all, it harmonized with the wishes, and possibly suggested the purpose, of the slave interest to pervert the great powers of the national government to the support of the inherently weak and tottering cause of slavery. Men who, to justify the fugitive slave law, had insisted, before the people, that the Constitution sanctions and protects slavery, and that such protection was one of the great purposes of the Constitution, could not well resist the logical application of the argument, when it was demanded by the slave interest, that the general government should, in *other respects, also, extend and protect slavery.* Their arguments returned to plague the inventors. What the ruling men of the Slave States most cared for, was this further use of the argument ; but some, even of these, condemned the obvious fallacy.

The Charleston *Mercury* in 1855, said, of the fugitive slave law :

"It was, from the first, a miserable illusion ; and worse, in fact, for it was an infringement of one of the most cherished principles of the Constitution, which provides that fugitives from labor ' upon demand shall be delivered up,' but gives no power to Congress to act in this affair. The tenth amendment to the Constitution provides that 'the powers not delegated to the United States are reserved to the people.' The clause above confers no power, but is the naked declaration of a right ; and the power not being conferred, results to the States as one of the incidents of sovereignty too dear to be trusted to the general government. Our southern members strove for the passage of the law, and strove honestly ; but it shows the evils of our unfortunate condition, that in the urgency of our contest with an aggressive adversary, we lose the landmarks of principle—to obtain an illusive triumph, we pressed the government to assume a power not conferred by the instrument of its creation, and to establish a precedent by which, in all after time, it will be authorized to assume whatever right may have no constitutional organ of enforcement."

But politicians who strove to pervert the general government to the support of slavery, and others, more logical, like the editors of the *Mercury*, who early appreciated its utter incompatibility with slavery, and yet held to slavery and advocated disunion, naturally came together, when the purposes of the former class had failed, and when republicanism was obviously about to resume its rightful sway in the conduct of our government. Probably the rebellion developed more successfully, and gathered more friends to its support, than if all who labored in its interest, had, from the beginning, adopted the logical conclusions of the *Mercury*.

We have not yet outlived the generation of politicians among us who, to keep the road to preferment open before them, substantially adopted, in both of the then great parties, the Shibboleth that *the Constitution means Slavery*. Many, even now, seem to hope for political salvation by its repetition. They who think there is any truth in the idea should reëxamine the Constitution, not in the false light of this doctrine, but in the clear light of the doctrine by which the Constitution was made — the doctrine of *the rights of man*. The unprejudiced and logical examiner will find there no sanction for slavery; much less will he find embodied provisions there for its protection and perpetuation. Men and States that permitted slavery were, indeed, by the Constitution, bound together with other men and States, in a general government. This fact of course shows that it was possible and permitted that slavery should exist under it, at least for a time; but it does not show that the government, created by the Constitution, assumed any responsibility for such existence. Marriage with a diseased person does not necessarily sanction the disease. There are plain and positive provisions in the Constitution directly hostile to slavery; and its abundant and strong provisions for liberty and republicanism are not nullified, and were not intended to be nullified, by counteracting provisions for the protection, extension or perpetuation of slavery, and such counteracting provisions do not exist in the Constitution. That this is unquestionably so, is shown by the rebellion in which slavery has found it necessary to engage, against a government that was only carried on according to its principles. The assumed justification of the rebellion is, that our government does not protect slavery. The answer to this is, that it never was intended that it should; and that the government is conducted according to its Constitution.

Let us do slavery and its friends the justice to admit that, *if its perpetuation be indispensable,* their present course is not unreasonable. Our republican system, as correctly described by Mr. Calhoun, has been found practically inconsistent with the system of slavery. Slavery will not, and can not, long tolerate free speech, a free press, general education, equal laws, and other concomitants of republicanism; and, therefore, against a government framed and adapted to secure these, slavery was necessitated to rebel.

The provisions in the Constitution, applicable to slavery, are general, covering other cases of social relations, and are in and of themselves right, irrespective of slavery; and therefore it is both unnecessary and illogical to assume that our fathers really did what they were ashamed of, and carefully and strongly protected slavery, though ignoring and avoiding its name. The coolie trade, as well as the slave trade, may be prohibited and punished by congress; and the right to pursue over a State line and take back persons escaping from labor, is a general provision, applicable to an apprentice system, or to any other which a State may adopt, and is intended to throw upon the several States the responsibility of the relations in them between employer and employed, and not to commit the United States government to the special sanction or support of any particular system. It is mutual, and was intended, probably, as much to protect communities from the unwelcome influx of a degraded class, as to give to other communities opportunity to recover their escaping laborers. This is shown by the readiness with which the provision was adopted: for it was not — as has been wrongly represented — the result of protracted discussion or of compromise, but its idea was first introduced near the close of the four months' session of the convention, and it was soon adopted, and without opposition.* Like that other provision guaranteeing States against insurrection, its ultimate and normal effect must really be favorable to liberty and republicanism, and not to slavery; for thereby each State is shut up with the social consequences of its own acts, to the peaceable solution, with free discussion, of social questions. We say, unhesitatingly, that slavery can not thus live; and they who are conducting this rebellion evidently have the same opinion. Shut up

* See Madison Papers, pp. 1417 and 1456.

slavery with republicanism, in any State, guarantee the existence
of the latter, with peace and free discussion, and slavery cannot
long survive.

Not the nature or constitutional provisions of our government,
but our administration of it, has prevented, or, rather, retarded, the
abolishment of slavery. The democratic republicanism, essentially embodied in the Constitution, had to struggle for its own
development in administration; and in that struggle it unfortunately allied itself, to some extent, with slavery, on the ground
of State rights, then common to both. The alliance was continued for the sake of power, when both Slavery and Democracy
became "national." But Slavery and Democracy could not
jointly conduct the government, and that happened which always
must happen in the use of power acquired by unnatural combinations — the principles of one ally superseded those of the other.
Slavery would not, and, if we are right, it could not safely yield.
Democracy therefore ceased to direct the common movements
still made in its name, and, in modern times, the inspiring spirit
and purpose of the party called "Democratic," were, simply,
Slavery.

Our system of government is peculiarly adapted to territorial
expansion. But expansion being more practicable on the side
next the Slave States, acquisition has been made to involve the
question of slavery; and thus, again, has the normal development
of the republican character of our government been checked, and
slavery been adventitiously advanced. Such was the case when
the Louisiana territory was acquired.

Mistakes made by the opponents of slavery have also done not
a little to give slavery advantage in its contests with republicanism in our government. The sentiment of the people, naturally
responsive to liberty, has sometimes been appealed to, in be-
half of measures found to be inexpedient, or intended to advance the interests of a political party, otherwise objectionable.
When Missouri applied for admission to the Union, as a State,
it had been attached to us as territory for sixteen years. The
United States government during all that time ought to have prohibited slavery there, as it properly might. But when the territory had grown to *Statehood*, and the United States government
was about to part entirely with its jurisdiction over the subject,
it was unreasonable to require the incipient State to abolish that

slavery which the United States government had itself permitted, and thus encouraged; especially as other *States* judged and acted, each for itself, on the subject within their respective boundaries. It became apparent, also, that opposition to the admission of Missouri was seized on, and selfishly used, by the political party that had then lately been driven into an almost hopeless minority. Missouri was rightfully admitted; but the compromise through which it was done, and the contest that preceded it, were injurious to republicanism, and beneficial to slavery. Liberty had been driven from an assumed position, and had compromised for half a right, and impliedly, but not the less effectually, conceded to slavery the other half, and thereby slavery secured a new guaranty. The friends of liberty first undertook to keep out a State, which, under the circumstances, they ought not to have attempted; and then compromised, by accepting the exclusion of slavery from *part* of the United States territory, when it ought to have been excluded from the whole, without compromise.

Those friends of liberty also made a mistake, who subsequently attempted to engage congress in the general abolition of slavery. They undertook to do a right thing in a wrong way, and gave to slavery the advantage of successful resistance; and, worse still, allowed slavery to hold up before it the ægis of the Constitution, and were thereby themselves unwisely and unfortunately drawn into hostility to the Constitution. Thence many of a whole generation of our countrymen have learned to distrust and detest abolition, in every form, even such as Washington, Patrick Henry, Jefferson and Franklin advocated, and have learned, at the same time, to transfer "constitutional" reverence to slavery, even as advocated by Jefferson Davis, Toombs, Yancey and DeBow.

The annexation of Texas was another occasion on which many friends of republicanism were misled, and slavery was incidentally helped, by association with a measure right and beneficial in itself. The adaptation of our system of government to almost indefinite expansion, as suggested and anticipated in the first part of this treatise, is not universally admitted. A class of our statesmen, respectable in numbers and standing, have denied it; and have always opposed acquisition. Their extended ideas of the functions proper for our general government would not allow them to believe it applicable to enlarged territory. Only they who see in the several State governments the best means of providing for much the largest portion of the governmental wants of the people, can properly appreciate the adaptation of our system to expansion. Texas was desired by this class for great national reasons — for peace, for republicanism, for freedom; but Texas was also desired for slavery. Texas was acquired, and, undue prominence being given to the latter reason, again was slavery adventitiously advanced, acquiring more and more a national character. But when republicanism shall have resumed its proper supremacy in our system, it, and not slavery, will be seen to be national, and then will the wisdom of the reannexation of Texas also more fully appear.

An effective reason why slavery has frequently, in the conduct of our government, been benefited at the expense of republicanism, is, that republicanism was universally known and admitted to be the essential principle of our system, incorporated and guaranteed in every part of it, while it was equally well-known, and, until lately, as universally admitted that slavery was not. Hence, slavery, in its conscious weakness, instinctively guarded its life, and never willingly consented to what might in any way endanger itself. Peculiarities in conducting the war of 1812 illustrate this. That war was begun and carried on in the interests of republicanism; but we can now see that the holding back on the northern frontier — the failure to acquire and hold Canada — was the work of slavery. Slavery has known that it could live under our system only for a while; and, therefore, like a doomed invalid, it instinctively took to nursing itself, and, in this struggle for life, it has, at length, become a vampyre.

The revival of republicanism had become necessary, not only because of such misleading circumstances and errors of opinion as we have noted, but also because too many of our people had become indifferent to their political duties. They did not feel the same necessity for defending the interests of republicanism that the opponents of republicanism in this contest have long felt for defending and advancing the interests of slavery. The earnest and thoughtful anxiety which attended the beginning of our experiment of self-government, had too far yielded to a feeling of conscious security. Politics, regarded as a profession, were becoming degraded and degrading, and immediate success being more prized than permanent principles, acquiescence became the popular doctrine which seemed to clinch and secure the advancing requirements of slavery. The dark time for freedom was not when Texas was annexed — there were other reasons than slavery for that; it was not when the "compromise measures" were passed — the fugitive slave-law awakened reaction; it was not when the Missouri compromise was repealed — that repeal gave force and form to the reaction; but it was when parties, in 1852, acquiesced in all that had been done for slavery. It was time for republicanism to revive, or it must, ere long, have slept here the sleep of death. Its revival was neither northern, nor eastern, nor western; but it belonged to our people, and to the character of our government.

In no respect is this contest sectional, except as every great contest must be so. We have, indeed, fallen into the habit of speaking of "the South" and "the North"—of "the Southern States" and "the Northern States;" but that which is usually and really intended is not a geographical distinction, such as Washington deprecated. Geographical distinctions in our country, if they shall come to influence our politics, will be found to be between "the West" and "the East," "the Seaboard States" and "the interior," "the Atlantic States" and "the Pacific States;" rather than between "the North" and "the South." Try this matter and the truth will appear. Missouri is a slave State, and therefore is called a Southern State; Kansas, adjoining on the west, and no further north, is a free State, and therefore is classed with Northern States. So of California, though extending further south; but had it adopted slavery, it would have been called a Southern State; so would Oregon. Were Texas to exclude slavery it would become, in this parlance, a "Northern State." New Mexico, Arizona, Delaware, Maryland, and even Pennsylvania and Illinois, and, in short, any State in the Union, or that may hereafter come into the Union, while slavery exists, would follow the same rule.

Neither is this contest personal. Personal combinations of ambitious men doubtless there are, and have been; but without a basis, a broad and real basis, no man or combination of men could originate or sustain such a contest in this country as we witness. They who lead — even the chiefs — are mere accidents of the movement. Personal ambition doubtless operates with them as with most men, to make them aspire to leadership; but this has not caused the movement, and does not sustain it. There is no individual, and no dozen of individuals, who caused or who carry on this rebellion, and without whom it would not be. Were its prominent men all removed, the contest, using other men as its instruments, must proceed to its development or its catastrophe. The rebellion is a distinct, decided and almost tangible thing, moving consistently towards a definite purpose; and they who regard it as a mere personal conspiracy, fail to appreciate the real and greatest danger. It is no more a personal conspiracy of its leaders than our republican system is a mere happy thought of Washington. This fact is further made evident from its absorption of men, even of strong men, who long opposed and resisted. Stephens and Houston and Bell and Clemens are traitors and rebels, as well as Davis and Wise and Pickens and Rhett. Other men, also, are absorbed, whose birth, education and early associations would have guarded them from entering into conspiracies merely personal, but could not prevent them from being carried along by a great movement when they had once assented to its essential principle. Principles are stronger, and control the men.

The single postulate from which is inevitably deduced the course of these men and of all men sustaining or favoring the rebellion, is, *slavery must be perpetuated*. The one great principle which unites the true men of our country, is, *republicanism must be perpetuated*. This distinction is the solvent, and it is the only solvent, in these times and in this country, of the action of men, of combinations, and of sections.

The men who caused this rebellion, and who sustain it, are all, in our country, who believe in slavery—all whose political thoughts, interests, principles and purposes are identified with its maintenance. The misfortune of these men, everywhere in our land, was, that the time had come when slavery required a rebellion — when it must certainly begin to die unless it could successfully rebel against republicanism and its government. Let us give them the credit of having first done all that they could to make the revolution a peaceable one — to change the government by construction and administration. But here, again, it was their misfortune that the necessities of slavery on the one hand, and the settled republican principles of the great mass of our people on the other, *compelled them to be violent*. They had to be violent in the Senate, violent in the Territories, and, morally, even more violent in the Supreme Court. Hence, a republican people was aroused, and peaceable revolution became impossible.

Let us also recognize the wisdom of the conductors of the rebellion in rejecting all overtures of political men for a compromise. They understood the case better than did those who made such overtures, and rightly judged it better for all concerned, either that slavery should be separated from republicanism, and become independent and entirely dominant, or, that it should yield entirely, and permit republicanism to become dominant. As gently as possible does republicanism exercise its sway in our government as it is; and not the manner of its exercising this sway, but the fact that it does exercise it, and that slavery can not, is the real trouble.

That this rebellion is not sectional, but springs, rather, from hostile political principles, may be further shown by reference to antecedents of prominent men. Passing by early southern patriots, so uniformly known as republicans and opponents of slavery, we notice, in these times, many of southern birth and education who hold, nevertheless, and with consistency, to their integrity and republicanism. President Lincoln is by birth a Kentuckian; Gen. Frémont a Carolinian. The Charleston *Mercury*, conscious of the fact which we notice, and of its influence, set itself to the task of personal detraction, in language which betrays the effect' of the rebuke of such examples. We quote from its issue of May 18, 1861:

"MAJOR ANDERSON has thus been weaned from his country, and has known only a servile allegiance to a flag which gives him pay and rations! So SCOTT, a mercenary at seventy-five, knows not Virginia as a mother." * * * "SCOTT and ANDERSON and CASSIUS CLAY and ANDY JOHNSON and a few besides will enjoy, we fancy, but a brief season in the misrepresentation of Kentucky and Tennessee. These are not brethren — they never were brethren. They were always mercenaries, and will so continue to the end of the chapter."

The *Mercury* thus shows that its standard for "brethren" is slavery and its cause, and not nativity.

On the other hand, it is also noticeable that a considerable portion of the active and influential men, on the side of slavery and its rebellion, were born and educated at the North. Yancey, Slidell, Yulee, and Albert Pike may be mentioned as specimens of this class. The fact of which we speak was lately noticed, on the ground, by the correspondent of the London *Times*. He says:

"For out and out Southern notions, there is nothing in Dixie's land like the successful emigrant from the North and East."

A correspondent of the New York *World*, writing lately from Nashville, Tenn., says that the bitterest, most unreasonable, unrelenting secessionists there, are natives of the North, mostly of New England; and he adds:

"The Adjutant-General of the regular confederate army — Samuel Cooper — was born in New York. Brig.-General Ripley was born in Ohio; Pemberton in Pennsylvania: Whiting, Pike, Ruggles, and Blanchard in Massachusetts; French in New Jersey.

"Massachusetts furnishes as many generals for the rebel army as either Alabama or Mississippi, one more than Texas, as many as Florida, Arkansas and Missouri, all together, and lacking one of half as many as South Carolina. Of course these men were citizens at the South at the breaking out of the rebellion."

But northern men who advocate slavery, and sustain its rebellion, are not merely those who live in Slave States. There is scarcely a neighborhood in all the North where this may not be abundantly proved and illustrated.

A leading political paper at the capital of the State of New York, speaking of a correspondent's proposal of an apprentice system, says:

"It is to be compulsory and we presume hereditary. We are glad to hear it. 'If we cannot alter things, by Jove we'll change their names, sir.'" * * * "Call the blacks apprentices, double their work and tighten their compulsion, and all perhaps will be well again."*

And the same paper, after the bombardment of Fort Sumter, advised to resist the President's requisition of troops to put down the rebellion.†

In short, everywhere, and without regard to section, climate or productions, they who believe in human slavery and in government adapted to it, do, and they logically must, justify and, so far as they can, sustain this rebellion and the revolution which it attempts; for the obvious reason that the republican system established by our fathers is, in principle, hostile to slavery, and irreconcilable with the system which slavery necessitates.

* Albany *Atlas and Argus*, June 28, 1861. † Same paper, April 15, 1861.

We turn to the men on whom is devolved the duty of putting down the rebellion, arresting the threatened revolution, and sustaining our constitutional government.

In the former part of this essay, the personality of individuals and of political organizations, was purposely avoided, in order to avoid diverting attention from principles. This is still desirable; yet it is not practicable to treat properly of this crisis, without treating of the persons who are engaged in it. This will, therefore, be done directly and plainly, but not further than is deemed necessary in order properly to understand the great subject before us.

It is but just to the successive heads of the acquiescent administrations which preceded Mr. Lincoln's, to relieve them from a large share of the personal blame which has been laid upon them, and to charge it home, rather, upon the people themselves. Those men were not elected to resist the encroachments of slavery. Some who helped to elect them may have supposed that they would do so; but they had really no right to suppose so. Those candidates have proved, on the whole, fair representatives of the interest which has elected them; and Mr. Douglas, had he been elected, and lived to administer the government, could not reasonably have been more blamed for acting still further on the principle of acquiescence in whatever new claims slavery might have made during his administration. The point is this: that the people of this country, by their elections, do really direct its policy. When — and not before — the people had fully determined upon effecting a change, it was done. It was not Mr. Lincoln who effected it, but the people who, directly and indirectly elected him; and the great reason, now, why Mr. Lincoln is not and can not, in his administration, also be an acquiescent in the demands and wishes of the slave interest is, that he was not elected for that purpose, but *was* elected to stand up steadily and firmly against them.

It is comparatively easy for a president to do what he knows he was elected to do; but it would be a task, the performance of which is reasonably to be expected of no man — not even of a Jackson or of a Napoleon, under our system — to stand at the head of affairs in resistance to the purposes of those who placed him there.

Not James Buchanan, but the Cincinnati Convention of 1856, and the electors who ratified its proceedings, prepared for and necessitated the measures of his administration. To the candid observer appears a reasonable and harmonious consistency throughout. He was purposely elected to conciliate the slave interest; and, that the measures in which he was required to acquiesce were worse, even, than those in which his predecessors had been required to acquiesce, is chargeable, not specially to the individual, ready as he was for the required service, but to the advancing necessities of slavery. They who had seen his name associated with those of Mason and Soulé, in the Ostend Manifesto, had no right to be surprised at the character and conduct of his secession cabinet ; and it forcibly illustrates the truth which we would present, that after the election of 1860, even Mr. Buchanan became somewhat conservative of our republican system, and substituted, in his cabinet, Dix and Holt for Floyd and Thompson. Indeed, the transition of administration from Mr. Buchanan, as it was last conducted by him, to Mr. Lincoln, as it was first exercised by him, was attended by no sudden jar. It seemed almost too much like the continuance of one administration to be entirely agreeable to the special friends of either ; but it was conformable to the popular will.

The election of Mr. Lincoln to the presidency was undoubtedly an event of more than usual significance. They who opposed, as well as they who favored it, were right in attaching to it very serious importance; but it was the result of no fortuitous combination. It was the intelligent and intended act of the people, but it was not, therefore, the less closely connected with the outbreak of the rebellion. Whether the election of some other man — the continuance, for another quadrennial period, of an administration more acquiescent in the wishes of the rebellious interest — would not have postponed or modified the open rupture, is not now a very material question ; for we think nearly all will now agree — and, on this point, time and reflection will but make the unanimity more complete — that acquiescence was not a remedy for our threatened danger — that it never was the proper remedy ; nay, that it directly and largely aggravated the danger and difficulty which it postponed.

When the war broke out, renewed evidence was given that the destinies of the country are in the hands of the people. They rallied at once to the support of their government, with men and with means, everywhere, save where the alternative of rebellion had been taken, and where the State governments were in the control of the slave interest. The echo of the rebel guns which opened on Fort Sumter had scarcely died along the coast of Carolina before the nation was in arms. The administration of the national government scarcely uttered its call, before the people responded, with numbers and amounts almost embarrassing. These resources would have sooner come, if sooner called. When the *Star of the West* was fired on, and when, afterwards, the project was considered of withdrawing or of reinforcing the garrison in Fort Sumter, had the Administration asked for forces, and shown an unhesitating determination to use them, forces in abundance would have come; and when, finally, they began to be collected, had it been the policy of the Administration to use them immediately to enforce the laws and suppress insurrection, there might have been greater and speedier demonstrations of national power. It was then evident, as was already demonstrated and announced in the first part of this essay, that the national force, and nothing but the national force, would bring us salvation. Had this conviction been earlier received, and acted on with the utmost possible promptness by those at the head of our national affairs, the people would not have been wanting on their part; for they were in advance of their officials in willingness to apply the remedy suitable to the occasion — the only remedy which has proved, or which could prove, effective.

Notwithstanding all untoward circumstances, republicanism revived and reasserted itself. The national heart beat strongly, and the national arm nerved itself with power. Sentiments that were supposed to animate but a portion of the people, were found to be general; and neutrality, that had lately assumed to be popular, disappeared before the plainer distinctions of the right and the wrong. Greater than any testimony previously borne by our people to the capacity of man for self-government, is that which they now give; for, in all the passing events, the great and noticeable fact is, that *the people*, and not any great statesman or general, are saving their country and its institutions. Not unlike the behavior of a timid soldier in his first battle, have been the manœuvres of our political men. Gladly would they have parleyed, or shrunk from the contest — some, even, who, at a distance, had boastfully asked "who's afraid?" Men who had risen to positions of influence, by persistently opposing compromise with slavery, had, at

5

last, engaged themselves in attempting such compromise, and, warning their party, had said, openly:

> "If the Republican party and the Republican Administration assume and perform the duty, they will save themselves while they are saving the country. If they refuse to do it their adversaries will be the party of the country, and will claim the advantages of that position."*

Fortunately for the country and for mankind, principles were stronger than men. The case did not admit of compromise: the conflict was irrepressible, and the forces moved on to the trial, the question, too plain for future misunderstanding, being, *republicanism and its government, or slavery and its revolution ?*

As our people were willing, so was our system of government competent. There has been no occasion whatever for the anxious solicitude with which many have looked for deliverance from our troubles by some great man or some special wisdom. The way out of them was already clearly laid down by our fathers in our Constitution and laws — too plainly for misunderstanding or mistake. "The executive power shall be vested in a President of the United States of America" — he shall swear: "I will faithfully execute the office of President of the United States, and will, to the best of my ability, preserve, protect and defend the Constitution of the United States" — "The President shall be commander-in-chief of the army and navy of the United States, and of the militia of the several States when called into the actual service of the United States" — "he shall take care that the laws be faithfully executed." Such are the provisions of the Constitution. The laws correspond: and congress, when called, was prompt to supply all needed additions. The path of duty was plain before the Administration — as plain as it has ever been before any administration of any government. The politicians were uselessly officious who endeavored to contrive some method of avoiding the issue so plainly presented to those whose duty it was to administer the government; and the error of these latter was in hesitating to advance promptly in the path of the Constitution and the laws — in waiting for somebody else to do what the Constitution had devolved on the federal executive. They were not answerable for consequences. They were only answerable for duties. The

---

* Albany Evening *Journal*, February 11, 1861.

great error of all, next to that of the rebellion itself, has been too little faith in the practical excellence of our republican system of government. Passing events are wonderfully enlarging and confirming this faith; and, it is to be hoped that never again will the memory of our fathers be wronged, and the arm of our power be in any degree paralyzed by want of faith in the adequacy of the government which they bequeathed to us, and which we have so severely tried, and have not found wanting. Henceforth, we trust it will be universally believed — and not by our own people alone — that our national government may be, and should be, when required, the quickest, the strongest, the most energetic and enduring in the world.

But the administration of our government should not be blamed, exclusively, for what has been participated in, and even caused, by the people themselves. Public sentiment in the loyal States having shown itself harmonious now, in the purpose to sustain the government and put down the rebellion, some have wondered why it has not been more speedily done; and various and even conflicting reasons have been given for delay. Want of military discipline, want of officers educated to war, want of arms, and of ships, want of favorable weather, want of a policy in the administration, want of a definite purpose in regard to slavery — as some say, to crush it, or as others say, to preserve it — have been assigned as the reasons; but the true and more comprehensive reason is to be found in our past course of opinion and action. To the patient and candid appears a divine justice, even in events that we deprecate. Our political history and our political troubles constantly show forth the relation of cause and effect; and even the tardy manner in which we are compelled to struggle out of our present troubles, is due less to inherent necessity than to incumbrances created by ourselves.

In the conduct of affairs the nation, now, has to look for salvation to its executive head; but how, and for what, was that head selected? It can not be forgotten that it was specially chosen with a view to moderation. Four years before, the Republican party, standing boldly upon principle, fought an open political battle. Triumphant in argument, and sustained by all the demonstrations of fast occurring events, it yet failed then of attaining governmental control. As the election of 1860 approached, the clamor on the one hand against radical opinions, and the desire

on the other to avoid another defeat, led to much talk and endeavor to "unite the opposition." Moderation and conservatism
were much commended and favored; and the problem of securing these, and the support which they could bring, without aban-
donment of principles, was well solved by the selection and election of our present executive head. But the election over, these
things could neither be forgotten nor evaded. An election in this
country has a meaning; and, how much soever political men may
be charged with dereliction of principle, candor compels the admission that principles are, notwithstanding, generally observed.
Even James Buchanan did what he could for the interest and
power which elected him, and did substantially as he was expected to do. That such is the general rule, and that it is more
and more strictly observed among us, vindicates our republicanism, shows that the people do govern, and shows, too, that the real
responsibility for national weal or woe belongs to the people themselves. What, then, was reasonably to be expected by this nation
from the present executive? Not, indeed, that the policy of pre-
ceding administrations, in yielding implicitly to the dictates of
the slave interest, and the guidance of secessionists, should be followed; but, certainly, that the principles of republicanism should
be applied with moderation.

In the contest with Mr. Douglas for the senatorship in Illinois,
which did so much to give Mr. Lincoln his national reputation,
the particular charge against which he had most frequently and
anxiously to defend himself and his party, was, of radicalism —
of disregard of southern rights, in a desire to elevate the negro to
social equality. This charge was both made with pertinacity, and
repelled with care, because both men well understood that it was
regarded as an important matter by the people whose votes they
were seeking. Doubtless that contest, while it commended Mr.
Lincoln to the conservative men of the country, impressed still
more upon his own mind the conviction of necessity for moderation in applying the principles of republicanism; and not unreasonably may he now suppose that, to the prevalence of the same
opinion among the people, he owes his election as President of
the United States. As a true representative man, is he not, then,
bound to be moderate? and if he is so, even to a fault, upon
whom, more than upon the people themselves, rests the responsibility?

We can imagine how a bold man, coming when he did to the presidency, might have led the nation; and how prompt decision and action might have aided the popular judgment; and can see that nothing in our system of government stood in the way of such action; but the nation had carefully avoided choosing a bold man, and had thereby purposely imposed upon itself a Fabian, rather than a Napoleonic, policy. Had the election of 1860 been positive in its issues, instead of negative, a positive policy might reasonably have been expected. Among people still claiming to be loyal, both the friends and the opponents of the successful candidates, treated the success as negative. Prominent Republicans even hastened to offer compromise; the supporters of Mr. Douglas clamored "*peace — no coercion*," challenging a declaration of policy in order to oppose it, and only rampant rebellion was positive. Large numbers seemed to expect that Mr. Lincoln would do no more than Mr. Buchanan had done, when, in the gentlest possible manner, he dismissed traitors from his cabinet, and undertook to continue the government, ignoring rebellion. Under such circumstances the pretexts were treated with most distinguished consideration. All may now see how utterly insignificant they really were; that the crisis did not turn at all upon them, but that it was an unavoidable collision of great and organized forces — a contest for mastery between democratic republicanism, as embodied in our constitutional system, and slavery, with its now recognized necessities.

Yet, singularly enough, an imperfect consciousness of the truth, stayed the arms of the forces on the side of the right. This generation of our people has been assiduously educated into hatred of abolition. To fight against slavery seemed to them too much like engaging in forcible abolition, and, therefore, large numbers took arms under protest. They protested against any sympathy for the slave, or any denial of the master's "right" to continue slavery. They who have called on our government for a more vigorous and anti-slavery policy should remember how strong are the prejudices of a life-time, even among educated and reasoning people. They might see that the same selfish indecision between the right and the wrong, which nursed the rebellion into life, stayed the hands of the people at first, when vigorous force and decisive action should have suppressed it. The indecision of the executive was but the reflex of the previous indecision of the people.

But the educational influences of the times have been great and effective. Our government and our liberties being attacked, our people have been compelled to think of their defence, and what that defence requires. The actual necessities of republicanism and its government occupy their thoughts, which before were too much occupied with the clamorous demands of slavery. Not merely by the booming of cannon and the clash of arms, not merely by great national perils at home and abroad, but also by small and still voices, and through a thousand avenues of reason and affection, have patriotic convictions come to the minds and hearts of the people; and not greater is the contrast presented now, by our martial hosts, compared with our former peacefulness, than is presented in the change of our public opinion. There is no mistaking the character of the determined conviction becoming unanimous. The cob-web sophistries woven about us are broken and scattered to the winds; the principles of republicanism are restored to their legitimate ascendancy; men, previously blinded, see what really is the government founded by our fathers; they recognize their own duties, and resolve upon their performance; and, instead of shrinking and cowering under the denunciations and threatenings of slavery, they clasp their arms around the pillars of the republic, rejoicing in liberty and security.

Yet with many, very many of our people, no change of opinion was needed. The character of our government and the character of slavery were understood by them, substantially, as herein exhibited, and, therefore, the contest which we witness has not found them surprised or unprepared. To these it comes, indeed, not unattended by a kind of sad satisfaction, like a long breath of suspense relieved — even like the breaking of morning after a night of darkness.

Another large class of our people fall naturally and harmoniously into the ranks of the defenders of our republican institutions — our citizens from other lands. They came here because they are republicans. By all their sad and pleasant memories of the past, by all their bright hopes of the future, they must coöperate zealously and heartily to maintain the cause of the American republic, supported by the stout hearts and strong arms of its own people, against the assaults of the American despotism, seeking alliance and support from European monarchies. Their unanimity in doing so, is neither accidental nor preconcerted, but results from the natural operations of inherent causes, as reliable as the principles of human nature.

The yielding acquiescence in the encroachments of slavery, which has characterized the people of this country for many years, is justly attributable, in large degree, to their love of our republican government, paradoxical as the proposition may seem. Slavery seemed to them a part of our system. It has been called an *institution*. The governmental system itself they realized to be good; and they were deceived into acquiescence in the demands of slavery by the threatened danger to republicanism. It had become the standard method with politicians, in extorting acquiescence, to praise the Union and the Constitution; in so much, that when a speaker or an editor entered upon the subject, all knew at once that he meant *Slavery*. *The Union, the Constitution, and the enforcement of the laws*, practically interpreted, meant — *The Union*, to be preserved only by acquiescing in whatever terms the slave interest might demand; *the Constitution*, that is, the guarantees for slavery claimed to be in the Constitution; *the enforcement of the Laws*, that is, the enforcement of the Fugitive Slave Law.

But slavery, in striking at our republican system of government, has dissolved this illusion, and at once emancipated the masses of the people from the mental thraldom which held them while slavery seemed to them a part of our government. The very affection for our republican system which had caused them to seem friendly to slavery, made them its determined enemies, when slavery, in its doomed career, undertook to overthrow our government, and the error, which connected slavery with its preservation, is banished forever.

It would have been wise in the Administration of our government to take immediate and full advantage of this change — it should even have been anticipated. Yet, that the Administration was slow to trust to its reality and extent, was, as has been shown, the natural result of our antecedent history. The chance at that time, and the only chance, for arresting civil war, was to be found in an immediate and overwhelming array of national force; and not merely in its array, but in an unmistakable determination to use it immediately to suppress the insurrection. It

was useless and dangerous to intimate that United States officers
would not be appointed where they were not acceptable to the
disaffected, to treat with " distinguished consideration " governors
who refused or neglected to comply with sworn constitutional duties, or to substitute, in any other particular, the suggestions of
temporizing expediency, for the plain and positive injunctions of
the Constitution and laws.   These were wiser than any policy.
No countenance should have been given to the idea, by any hesitation implying choice, that resistance to insurrection was a policy ; but all should have been made immediately to see and feel
that it was a necessity — that it was the government of the United
States, and not a political party — the president of the United
States, and not Abraham Lincoln or his advisers — the laws of
the land, and not the policy of an Administration, that resisted
rebellion and revolution.   Forbearance was wasted on predeterm-
ined revolutionists.   It embarrassed, not them, but the government; encouraged spies and traitors everywhere, and naturally
led to the exercise, on other occasions, of doubtful and arbitrary
power.   Possibly it was then already, of necessity, a case in which,
without the shedding of blood — even of much blood — there
could be no remission of sins ; and yet, it seems possible that superior forces arrayed everywhere against insurrection might have
prevented a battle anywhere.   Meeting the enemies of our government so often with inferior forces, and especially in the contest
at Bull Run, insured the conversion of insurrection into civil
war ; and the tolerant policy of fighting rebellion gently, gave the
first real alarm to the staunch friends of our government, and
aggravated our national difficulties and dangers at home and
abroad.

    Yet this very policy has, in another aspect of results, afforded
to the country and to the world magnificent evidence of the recuperative power of our popular republican system.   Had the
man on whom devolved the duty of exercising the executive
power of the nation seen, in the beginning, as clearly as he probably now does, our great national resources, and the duty of using
them promptly, national salvation might have seemed to come
from the man, rather than, under Heaven, from the people themselves ; and history might have attributed the nation's survival
of the crisis to accidental or providential interposition, rather than

to the philosophical excellence of our governmental system, and the normal inspiration of a whole people.

Doubtful, and even disastrous, might have been the result, if our federal policy had been moulded at this time upon the preconceived ideas or temporizing suggestions of politicians, called, by their admirers, *great statesmen.* As it is, and despite a president justly credited for integrity of purpose, their schemes have doubtless wrought the country much mischief; not merely through the peculation and patronage attending enormous expenditures, but through the jealous rivalries that would obstruct national salvation. These things being part of the rationale of the crisis, mention of them is not improper, but their further consideration not being essential to the purpose before us, they are gladly dismissed.

We have seen what are the essential principles and character of our constitutional system of government, and, on the other hand, what are the necessities of slavery, and how naturally it has come to rebel against our government — have seen what is really the impelling power behind the persons who have advanced to represent and sustain the proposed revolution — have, also, glanced at some leading events in our political history affecting particularly the questions before us, and have considered somewhat the action of the men who support our government. Certain inferences flowing logically and inevitably from the facts and principles hereinbefore stated, demand our attention, and will now briefly be considered.

First. The length of the war depends, chiefly, upon the Federal Executive.

Second. The proper end and object of the war is, the restoration of the legitimate supremacy of the General Government throughout the land.

I. Regarding the first of these propositions, it has been shown that the contest being one of principles essentially irreconcilable, is necessarily a contest of forces — a trial of strength between republicanism and slavery. They who have failed to recognize this fundamental truth have failed, utterly and continually, to appreciate the magnitude and persistency of the contest. Recognizing the nature of the crisis, it was easy, a year ago, to prescribe the national force as the remedy for our national ailment. Looking then at the relative strength of the right side and of the wrong side in the contest of force, it seemed easy, also, to foresee which must prevail. But the result of a contest depends upon the forces used, rather than upon the forces possessed. Many reasons have herein been given, and many more must have suggested themselves to the thoughtful reader, why those engaged in this rebellion would put forth their strength promptly and fully. They understood the rationale of this crisis sooner and better than those did whom they opposed; and, when they resolved on rebellion, had already emancipated themselves from conscientious restraints. In this they were helped by their known inferiority of real strength, and it was because they expected to use a greater relative proportion of their strength, and to use it faster, that they counted, nevertheless, upon success. They believed that the supporters and representatives of republicanism, less earnest than the supporters and representatives of slavery, would hesitate to use force, and would cling rather to peace and acquiescence. Many of the false hopes with which loyal people have deluded themselves as to the failure, diversion, or arrest of the rebellion, were exposed in our earlier pages. Experience is demonstrating not only that it could not and would not stop of itself, or be arrested, save by the exercise of superior national force, but that its power, in men, money and means, was not insignificant. They who thought otherwise forgot that *all* the possessions of slavery were necessarily staked on success; and that the rebellious interest being strong enough in a given section of country to start on its career, could not and would not afterwards wait for volunteers. They forgot the essential nature of military despotism into which the whole people of that section were inevitably plunged by the first rush, and that, by allowing headway to the rebellion, every man and every dollar within its reach were subjected to its control.

A Savannah (Georgia) correspondent wrote to the Richmond (Virginia) *Despatch* :

"Our citizens (the few who remained) have been arrested on the street, dragged to camp, shown a tent, and informed that there their habitation should be. And this has been done by a parcel of beardless boys, who have been mustered into the State service."

This specimen accords with the system which we know, from the nature of the case, must prevail wherever the rebellion dominates. Even Union strength counts for the rebels where they, and not we, can appropriate it. To their power of coercing all nominally free people within their reach to contribute goods, services, and life to sustain the rebellion, must be added, also, that which they have long possessed and exercised -- the power to extort their living, in the mean time, from the labor of their slaves. Still another great element of power at the service of any enemy of our republicanism, is, the hostility of other and anti-republican governments. Slavery knew this, and did not omit to prepare in time to secure its full advantages.

The correspondent of the Charleston *Mercury*, in the letter from which some extracts have already been given, written from Washington, January 11, 1857, when Mr. Buchanan was about making up his cabinet, says:

"The representatives from the Continental Powers are studious in their attentions to southern Senators and Representatives, and it is to be hoped the interest will be returned with a good will. We should seek, by all the means in our power, to promulgate, through these official sources, the principles and ideas of the South.

"It would be very desirable, even if our politicians were to lend their influence in favor of the Continental party in Europe, by having the right sort of men at the most important points, commercial and diplomatic. The elements contending for admission into Mr. Buchanan's cabinet here indicate how watchful and earnest the South should be in this crisis." * * * * * * * * *

"We may accomplish a great deal, however, by building up alliances and friendships on the Continent of Europe. We may, through proper coöperation, do much, very much, for ourselves abroad."

The hasty recognition of the rebels as belligerents, by the two nations of Europe who could be most dangerous to ours, shows that these precautions of slavery were not fruitless. Not the least of the foolishness and wickedness of our past Administrations, and of the people who sustained them, has been the sending to other nations of anti-republican men, as the representatives of our nation. The inherent hostility of anti-republican governments to our own, as illustrated by the conduct of European nations at this time, is a marked and significant feature of this crisis; but its full consideration would require more space than can here be spared. It was wisely calculated on as an effective ally of the rebellion against our republican government, and this we would doubtless more fully have learned to our cost, if the demonstration of our vitality and force had been but a little longer delayed. Added to the other resources of the rebels, the possible advantages which they might derive from this, would make an array of force against our government greater than has generally been supposed possible.

But, on the other hand, there seems to have been even a greater failure to appreciate the national force which could be opposed to rebellion. The nature of the contest being such as we see, the whole resources of the people of the republic, counting every man and every dollar, and including even the rebellious districts, as fast as they could be reached, are, by the nature of the case, pledged to the support of our republican government against any and all of its enemies. We have, as has been shown, a government fully organized, capable of applying these resources to any needed extent. The will to use them to the needed extent undoubtedly exists in the people, and, though slow in its manifestations, it exists, also, in the Administration of our government. How great this power really is, we may not now know, and the world may never know; but if, by demonstration, it shall ever be known, the world will be astonished at its magnitude. Unwisely, in this contest, many have been seeking the limitations of our national power. They can only be found by trial; and this contest, great as it is, can not even approximate to its measurement. Had England and France joined hands with slavery against our republicanism, and had our Government, responding to the sentiments of the people, rallied for the contest, the array against us, including all whom those two great nations of Europe, with their navies, could bring to our shores, would, even then, have been no cause for despair. Necessity is the rule and the only limitation in military defence by a republic, as well as by other governments; and in circumstances sufficiently urgent, not only our four millions of white men, capable of bearing arms, but another million, also, of our darker brethren might then be deemed worthy to strike with us the enemies of republicanism.

Our numerical force, our isolation as the masters of a continent, our grain-producing facilities and extended territory, are by no means our only, and scarcely are they our distinguishing, advantages. Man for man, there has never existed, anywhere, a people capable of being so terribly dangerous in war. They have, it is true, been addicted rather to the arts and the policy of peace. But they are wonderfully inventive and versatile. The old art of war is, in these days, subjected to rapid changes under the influence of invention and improvement. Make war the great market for American invention and enterprise, and new developments would be given to destructive power, before which the prestige of the human machinery of standing armies and the prowess of old navies would wane. Already has this been illustrated to such extent in this war as to attract attention from abroad, and to raise the question among ourselves, whether our own military and naval systems are not too antiquated, and to suggest comparisons of effective results not always favorable even to those whom our country has specially educated to war. In the old art of the organization and movement of armies, the men of this country have advantages. They are trained in organization. Our political organizations, our voluntary religious organizations, our industrial, educational, eleemosynary, artistic, and social organizations, in which our people so generally participate, make the business of organization familiar to all; and, as necessity requires, the same people readily and handily apply its principles to war. They make good soldiers and good officers, because they understand their mutual duties and obligations. Not years, and scarcely months, are required to give to their movements and discipline the perfection usually predicated only of veterans; and, impatient of domination as *sovereigns* are supposed to be, American soldiers do not mutiny. Not satisfied with cheerful conformity in essentials entrusted to Government, our people, through voluntary associations, afford effective assistance in incidental and important details. Witness the Sanitary Commission, guarding the health of our soldiers, nursing the sick and the wounded, and demonstrating that our women, as well as our men, can, by making it more useful and effective, greatly augment the national force.

But the occasion which we have supposed as possibly most trying to our national force, can never come unattended by other great elements of power. Our traditional policy, according, also, with our principles, is peace. Other nations will never have opportunity to attack us, even when we may be taken at a disadvantage, except by placing themselves in the wrong. In such a war, waged against us by even two or three of the most powerful nations of Europe, we should stand as the representatives of republicanism for the world; and the growing republicanism of the world would help us. The cause of our Federal Union would be the cause of oppressed nationalities everywhere, and the cause of our people would be the cause of man. We are already too big and strong to be crushed out of existence at once. Our seaboard cities and exposed positions might be taken or destroyed; but, ere the life of the nation could be touched or greatly endangered by the combined despots and aristocracies of the world, they would be called home to defend their own possessions. No; it is too late in the history of the world for outside enemies successfully to attack our American republicanism. If true ourselves to its principles, their array against it would seem like the signal for the last great conflict — "the Armageddon of the world."

Such being our national power and capability, notwithstanding the array against us, little more is needed to establish the first proposition of our conclusion. That force is the proper remedy for the rebellion, is demonstrated now by experiment, and it was morally certain before. A power, too great and dangerous to be despised or disregarded, is arrayed against us, and it will certainly yield to nothing but the actual cogency of a greater power. We have that greater power, and, though it is capable of long endurance, all the economies urge us to use it quickly. Our force is abundant, our government is competent, our people are willing. The executive department of our government is purposely organized and adapted for such use. It is the nation's agent for the exercise of the nation's force. It has the simplicity and directness of a single head, and within its legitimate sphere, which certainly includes this case, it may, congress supplying the means, have all the effectiveness which any government can ever have — even were it a monarchy or a despotism. Not the vigorous exercise of executive power, but the neglect to exercise it now, would be unconstitutional. Allowing only the time necessary for the production of results, we must infer, therefore, that the length of the war depends, and has from the beginning depended, upon the Federal Executive.

II. They who have had the patience carefully to follow our course of investigation, and especially all who agree substantially with the statement of principles herein, will find little difficulty in agreeing, also, that the proper end and object of the war is the restoration of the legitimate supremacy of the General Government throughout the land.

In the beginning, they who did not see the way clear for the restoration of the United States authority, in all the States, were sufficiently numerous to give just cause for anxiety, on account of the dangers which might, at such a time, result from divided counsels. Their incipient plans and suggestions for separation and reconstruction were exceedingly mischievous. Few doubt now; and nearly all agree that the federal authority must everywhere be restored. But all do not agree that this is enough. Some, reacting from the alarm which first made them despair of the integrity of the Republic, and others, anxious to seize what they deem a rare and most favorable opportunity, would direct the action of the General Government against slavery, as the *cause* of the rebellion. If the facts and inferences in these pages be correct, slavery undoubtedly is the cause of the rebellion and the war; but it is in such sense the cause, as a defective organization or constitutional tendency is often the cause of crime in an individual. Wise public authorities do not, in such case, punish the tendency. They punish the criminal; and encourage moral agencies for the reformation of the tendency.

Slavery is, for reasons which we have given, and which might be enlarged and multiplied, a dangerous element in a republic. It is bad for any government or any people, and its principle, as has been shown, is utterly irreconcilable with republicanism. That it must certainly cease, in each and every of these United States, is as certain as that our people are wise—as certain as that God is just. But that its immediate cessation in every State is necessary to the life and development of the republic is disproved by years of general republican prosperity, while it has continued. It must, of course, be conceded, that if its existence for a time in some of the States will lead to its perpetuation and extension, and so to the destruction of republicanism, then its immediate and utter extermination is a necessity; also, that if, in the present war, or in any other that may occur, proclamation of immediate freedom for all, should become necessary in order to cripple our enemy, or to bring us needed allies, it should be made, and should be sustained by our national power; and this on the principle that the safety of the people is the highest law. But if, on a fair examination and understanding of our political system, it clearly appears that we possess therein, and through its normal action, abundant and certain means of resisting all encroachments of slavery, and also abundant and certain means of suppressing rebellion, even this rebellion for slavery, then it does not appear

that the proper remedy for this rebellion, or the proper method
of avoiding similar calamities in the future, consists in the use of
abnormal means, or in changing or modifying our system of government: and if, in addition, we can plainly see that our present
tribulations are chargeable to ourselves — to our own selfishness,
corruption and neglect, and not to the system of government fur-
nished us by our fathers, it would obviously be a self-deceptive
blunder to tinker the system.

Notwithstanding the relation of cause and effect existing between slavery and the rebellion, in the sense herein explained, it
is easy to conceive of, and to treat, the one abstractly from the
other. This rebellion, caused by slavery, should be treated by
our Government substantially as rebellion against our government
arising from any other conceivable cause should be treated. It
should be crushed; and the men engaged in it should be punished by our General Government *for being engaged in rebellion*,
and not for their connection with slavery.

On the other hand, there is no obligation resting on our Government to proceed gently with the rebellion, on account of slavery. Slavery has, as has been shown, no guaranties in our constitution, the guaranties claimed for it being general guaranties
for States or for people, and which are right and proper in themselves, independently of slavery; and slavery being, in and of itself, a wrong, it can claim no moral rights whatever. Unhesitatingly, therefore, should our Government advance in the suppression of this rebellion. Having itself no care or responsibility whatever for slaves as such, the United States Government
is not to be expected, and should not be persuaded to try, to preserve their character of slaves, when, in the performance of its
military duty of suppressing the rebellion, it goes, with its officers
and soldiers, into territory where slavery has been recognized and
protected by State governments. The men, and *all* the men,
whom it encounters there, are to be recognized and treated as men
— as loyal or rebellious, as friends or as enemies, accordingly as,
through their own personal conduct, they respectively deserve;
and if, in the absence or abeyance of State jurisdiction over the
social relations of the inhabitants, the United States Government
has, through its military force, and during its military occupation,
to assume the regulation of social relations, it should undoubtedly
do so, on the principles of right, and not on the principles of wrong

—on the principles of liberty, and not on the principles of sla
very. The United States Government temporarily administering
social and local government in South Carolina, has no more obligation or right to engage in, or to countenance slavery, than it
would have, during military occupation of the Feegee Islands, to
engage in, or to countenance, cannibalism.

Much has been said of the moral obligations of the United
States Government to protect the "rights" of loyal slave owners
residing among disloyal people. The answer to this is two-fold :
first, as slave owners, these people have no *moral* rights, and,
therefore, towards them, as such slave owners, the United States
Government is under no moral obligations ; and, *secondly*, if not
their fault, it is at least their misfortune, that their State Governments, under which only, their *legal* "right" to hold slaves was
secured, have failed in their functions. They held their slaves
subject to this risk. The United States Government is under no
obligation to indemnify them. But in States where the social
relations of the people are still under the peaceful jurisdiction of
the State authorities, the United States forces can not properly
interfere.

This subject will be more fully understood by referring to the
character and nature of our respective governments. The United
States Government, though of limited jurisdiction, is nevertheless
a *government*, and is the only war-making or war-conducting government which we constitutionally have. There is no constitutional authority whatever for the war now being carried on in
this country, except as it is carried on on the part of the
United States Government. As a military governmental power,
the United States Government may, most undoubtedly, administer local government wherever it may be required by military
necessity, and also where, during the abeyance or demoralization
of any State Government, by reason of war, the inhabitants of any
State or locality belonging to the United States, might otherwise
suffer for want of governmental protection. This temporary local
government by the United States may be either with or without
the formal declaration of martial law. But the United States
Government has no right or constitutional power to establish or
maintain slavery in the course of such local government. Moreover, government by military law is government by force. Slavery, also, is maintained by force. But two separate systems of

6

force can not harmoniously prevail at the same time, in the government of the same locality. The United States must, in such case, have entire control over all the inhabitants of such locality, with power to punish each individual for his own wrong acts, and can not safely permit that absolute control of individuals by others which is necessarily implied by the system of slavery. Therefore, constitutionally and by necessity, the United States Government can not, in administering local government, undertake to sustain slavery. Slaves, therefore, become free in such locality, not so much because the United States Government does anything directly to make or declare them free, as *because there is no longer any governmental authority to hold them as slaves.* The United States Government simply treats them as men, to be dealt with by its military government as necessity, humanity and duty may dictate. It can not effectively declare them " forever free," because, its local government being only temporary, the State Government, on resuming its functions, may reduce them again to slavery. But the United States Government may undoubtedly do as it has already assumed to do, in certain cases, by law of congress, extinguish entirely the claim which a rebellious individual may have to the services of another individual, so that that claim can no longer stand under State law, or any law, as the sanction for further enslavement of the person thus freed.

According to these principles there is no more difficulty, and there should be no more embarrassment, in the United States Government's performing its functions in the slave States, than in its performing them in the free; and, certainly, there should be no more embarrassment in the necessary military occupation of South Carolina, than there was in the military occupation of Mexico. In both cases, local regulations and usages, not in their nature wrong — not conflicting with the rights of man — and not hostile in their character, should, doubtless, be respected; but those falling within these exceptions can properly claim no aid from the occupying power. In other words, the United States Government, having neither rights nor obligations in respect to slavery in the slave States, is as free to exercise its military authority in them, as in the free States, in doing whatever may be proper and effective to suppress the rebellion; but, being under both moral and constitutional obligations to treat all men justly, it can not without gross wrong and inconsistency, assume, during temporary military occupation of any State, any of the functions peculiar to a Slave Government. To do so, would be voluntarily and gratuitously to participate in the wickedness of enslaving men.

The embarrassments in some minds on this subject have, doubtless, grown out of the mischievous fallacy, having, itself, a modern and fungous growth, that slavery is, in some way, under the protection of the United States Government. It is not so; *States* and *people*, where slavery may exist, are under the protection of the United States Government; but slavery is solely dependent upon State protection, save, till lately, in the District of Columbia and some other places, where the comity of the United States Government has been extended to cover wrong. When the people of slave States rebelled, and thus invited military occupation of their territory by United States forces, they voluntarily subjected their darling " institution " to exposure, stripped of governmental protection. Let them take the consequences. Neither the loyal people of the United States nor the United States Government can justly be called on to assume for them any part of the responsibility. To the Government it should not be of the least consequence that slavery may greatly suffer in the course of, and in consequence of, suppression of the rebellion; and to the people it should be just cause of congratulation, that a stupendous wrong is writhing under the wheels of the advancing car of the Almighty. The moral sense in which slavery stands in the relation of cause to this war, justifies the people now, and will forever hereafter justify the historian in rejoicing that calamity has, in this case also, attended wrong.

The measure of that calamity will inevitably be great, and beyond what the most comprehensive human understanding can now calculate. In the popular estimation — which is controlled always by moral considerations — slavery stands already, everywhere, as the cause of this rebellion. Its mere failure of success destroys its political prestige. When it was supposed to elect our presidents, it was feared and respected, even if disliked. Henceforth, and perpetually, till its last vestige shall disappear from the land, it must carry with it the burden and disgrace of this wicked war against " the best government on earth," and of the disastrous and utter failure in which its war must inevitably terminate, on the mere restoration of our legitimate national supremacy. Our legislative halls, our deliberative assemblies, our churches, our hustings, our streets, fields and homes, must continually reëcho with the story of its deep damnation.

The war will greatly have affected the slaves themselves. Numbers of them will have become practically free beyond the possibility of reënslavement, and in the minds and hearts of all, thoughts and aspirations will have been introduced and stimulated, preparing and leading them towards a change which, sooner or later, must surely come. They will have seen their masters vanquished, and this, of itself, means much. It is a lesson that no time can erase, and no blind conceal. Wise masters will know the lesson also, and ponder it thoughtfully; and their wisdom will, we are confident, not be without useful results. The desolations spread by the war over the slave States will be lasting and terrible remembrancers, drawing upon slavery the curses of the people. The millions of money that must annually be contributed in taxes to pay the interest and principal of the war debt, are items in the account which this and coming generations will charge against slavery. And, more than all, mourning for the dead, saddening the hearts of the living, will, in every neighborhood, and almost in every family through the land, especially in the slave States, call slavery to the bar even of human judgment. The non-slaveholders of the slave States, on whom this burden has already fallen fearfully, can scarcely fail to ask themselves, and then, also, to ask their leaders: for what good have they been led into this slaughter? Slavery would not, in the past, bear questionings. These are questionings which it can not now escape. Ignorance has long closed the eyes and the ears of the people where slavery exists; but some things, even the blindest eyes have now seen, and the deafest ears heard.

They who fear that restoration of the legitimate authority of the United States Government throughout the land will prove inadequate to the security and peace of the republic, can not have sufficiently considered what, and how much, this necessarily means. It is a commanding of the peace in every State and Territory. This is one of the great and peculiar functions of the Federal Government, and the whole force of the nation is pledged to its constant maintenance. It is also the restoration of State government, in every State, to the care and administration of loyal men. The remark near the close of the first part of this exposition, to the effect that State governments would not be put into the hands of minorities, must be understood as referring to possible majorities, more or less disaffected, perhaps, but not yet outlawed by rebellion. The Constitution of the United States provides (Art. 6): "The members of the several State legislatures, and all executive and judicial officers, both of the United States and of the several States, shall be bound by oath or affirmation to support this constitution." Men who refuse to take such oath can not properly be recognized by the United States Government as State officers. By the same article it is declared that the United States constitution, laws and treaties "shall be the supreme law of the land; and the judges in every State shall be bound thereby, any thing in the constitution or laws of any State to the contrary notwithstanding." When physical resistance to the United States authority is overcome in any State, it can not be difficult to recognize the loyal citizens. The disloyal, they who, by active rebellion, unrepented of and unatoned for, have abdicated their citizenship, have no more right to control the State, or even to share in the management of its government, than alien enemies, who, having made a descent upon any State, should set up a claim to control it. If, by insurrection and war, the machinery of any State government has become disorganized, the loyal people of the State, protected, and, if need be, assisted, by the United States Government, can readily restore it. Restoration of the legitimate authority of the United States Government means, therefore, the restoration of loyal State Governments and authority, executive, legislative, and judicial.

Thus the governmental system established by our fathers, shown to be inherently democratic republican, and proved by experiment to be not adapted to slavery and its necessities, becomes reestablished in every State, backed by the whole force and authority of the General Government to sustain it. That this condition can not possibly be made sufficiently to subserve the purposes of slavery, is proved by the rebellion against it. Rebellion was a necessity for slavery, because it could not maintain itself without. It had, before, exhausted every means of perverting our government as it is, to the subservience of its necessities. The election of Mr. Lincoln showed that republicanism was inevitably to resume its legitimate sway; and that slavery had only the alternative, on the one hand, to submit — to subside from na-

tional domination, and to contend with republicanism in the several States, sure to be gradually overcome there, also — or, on the
other hand, *to rebel*. It chose the latter; and, failing in this, it
will be thrown back again upon the other alternative, and under
far greater disadvantages than before, crippled, disgraced, ab-
horred.

Regard for State sovereignty and State rights was wisely developed in this country, and the philosophical teachings of our early
southern statesmen contributed largely to such development. But
it is a mistake to suppose that regard for this doctrine now char-
acterizes the slave States. As perverted by the slave interest, it
had, for some time previous to the rebellion, been used only as a
kind of fetch to sanction aggressions of slavery, and to oppose republicanism in the General Government. The uniform course of
Senators and Representatives in congress from the slave States,
with regard to Kansas, and of all northern men under their influence, clearly shows this.

For further illustration, and also to show further the inherent
and conscious hostility of slavery to republicanism, we give here
certain propositions, regarded as fundamental, introduced by Mr.
Collier, as a joint resolution, May 15, 1862, into the senate of the
pretended Confederate State of Virginia :

"The General Assembly of Virginia doth hereby declare, that negroes in slavery
in this State and the whole South (who are, withal, in a higher condition of civilization than any of their race has ever been elsewhere), having been a property in their
masters for two hundred and forty years, by use and custom at first, and ever since
by recognition of the public law in various forms, ought not to be, and can not justly
be, interfered with in that relation of property, by the States, neither by the people in
convention assembled to alter an existing Constitution, or to form one for admission
into the Confederacy, nor by the representatives of the people in the State or the Confederate legislature, nor by any means or mode which the popular majority might
adopt, and that the State, whilst remaining republican in the structure of its government, can lawfully get rid of that species of property, if ever, only by the free consent of the individual owners, it being true, as the General Assembly doth further
declare, that for the State, without the free consent of the owner, to deprive him of
his identical property, by compelling him to accept a substituted value thereof, no
matter how ascertained, or by the *post nati* policy, or in any other way not for the
public use, but with a view to rid the State of such property already resident therein,
and so to destroy the right of property in the subject, or to constrain the owner to
send his slaves out of the State, or else to expatriate himself and carry them with him,
would contravene and frustrate the indispensable principles of the government ; and,
whereas, these Confederate States being all now slaveholding, may be disturbed by
some act of the majority, in any one of them, in derogation of the rights of the minority, unless this doctrine above declared be interposed ; therefore,

"*Resolved, by the General Assembly of Virginia,* That the Governor of Virginia be, and he is hereby, requested to communicate this proceeding to the several Governors of the Confederate States, and to request them to lay the same before their respective legislatures, and to request their concurrence therein in such way as they may severally deem best calculated to secure *stability to the fundamental doctrine of southern civilization, which is hereby declared and proposed to be advanced.*"

It will be seen that that, against which this resolution is particularly directed, is, control over the subject of slavery *by the people of a State.* It is proposed to guard "the fundamental doctrine of southern civilization, which is hereby declared" by interposing this doctrine above deduced, lest the "Confederate States, being all now slaveholding, may be disturbed by some act of the majority, in any one of them, in derogation of the rights of the minority." There is nothing here of State rights or of popular sovereignty; but, on the contrary, a careful guarding against State action or control, and against the people — "the majority," either in convention assembled to alter or to form a constitution, or by State legislation, or "by any means or mode which the popular majority might adopt."

An immediate vote on the resolution was not requested, and, accordingly, the subject was laid over; but the mover, in the carefully considered remarks which accompanied his introduction of the resolution, fully confirms our deductions as to the principles involved in this rebellion. He says: "It is the repudiation of this doctrine that is at the top and bottom, and in all the circumference, of the struggle in which we are engaged," and that, if this doctrine be not sound, slavery ought to be, and will be, abolished. He is right, also, as we have already shown, in believing that the true way to secure slavery from all disturbance or interference, is to leave it, not to the States nor to the people of the States, but to the voluntary action of slaveholders; but he is, we think, unnecessarily diffident as to the reception of his doctrine in a Slave Confederacy. It is the doctrine which will certainly be acted on, whether avowed or not, by the controlling interest in this rebellion. We quote from his remarks as reported :

"His reason for forbearing to ask a vote at this time, he said, was, that he did not believe the public men of the South appreciated the doctrine announced. They do not appreciate it at its vital and most valuable point, which is its denial of the power of the majority, in making a constitution for a State, to disturb a preëxisting and resident property. The prevalence of this doctrine in the intelligence of the world can alone give the slaveholding States exemption from war. It is the repudiation of this doctrine that is at the top and bottom, and in all the circumference of the struggle in which we are engaged. If the principal sentiments asserted in that declaration, and from which the doctrine proposed as the practical result is educed, be not sound in the philosophy of the subject, and ought not to be adopted into the public law, then negro slavery ought to be abolished, and Divine wisdom will accomplish the deliverance. But, he said, he did believe the sentiments sound and the doctrine logically inevitable, and that negro slavery will exist in the countries governed by the white race until the native land of the black man shall have been civilized and Christianized. Mr. Collier said he would only now add the desire that every newspaper in the Confederacy, and as many elsewhere as will, would publish that declaration."

Seeing what doctrine the rebellion requires for its support, we may better understand, by contrast, the excellence of the doctrines embodied in our popular constitutional system; and that the rebellion, if successful, would entirely subvert them in both the State and the General Governments.

There is no necessity now, for additional safeguards for our General Government against slavery. Our system as it is, enabled the people, when they desired to do so, to oust slavery from its control, and to restore republicanism. When the rebellion, which slavery thereupon initiated, is suppressed, republicanism and its governmental system will be safe. Only culpable neglect by the people themselves can endanger either; and against the consequences of such neglect, there can be no reliable safeguard, and it would not be well for the people themselves if there could. If this war were attributable to our system of government, or to its want of any constitutional safeguards, the case would be different. We can see clearly that, not the system, but the past administration of it, was defective; and that the system itself affords abundant remedies. Dangers overcome are no longer dangers.

The right, and even the duty, of the General Government, if necessary, to arm and use as soldiers, against the national enemies of whatsoever kind, negroes who may have been held as slaves under State laws, can not properly be disputed. It is a right which should be unhesitatingly exercised, and to its fullest extent, rather than submit to national destruction; but considering our abundant national strength, the necessity to employ them as soldiers is not likely to occur at this time, except, possibly, to a limited extent, in districts where, for a season, the lives of unacclimated troops would be otherwise endangered. The right, also, to extinguish any claim of rebels to personal services of other men, and to confiscate their property as punishment for treason, and towards indemnity for national expenses, caused by the rebellion, can not be successfully disputed. Slavery should be no shield or safeguard for the rebellion; and should afford not the least indemnification against condign punishment of the patricidal enemies of the republic.

But the rights here claimed can not properly be used as pretexts; and if they could, they could not be made effectual, permanently to liberate the slaves in any State, allowing them to remain there, without so altering the United States constitution as to confer upon the General Government the power to protect and perpetuate their freedom. According to our system and Constitution as they now stand, the condition of the various classes of inhabitants of each State, is matter for State regulation. This was one of the reasons for removal of the Indians from within State limits.

Some would suggest pursuing a similar policy with the negroes. This would be an immense undertaking, and seems neither wise, nor timely, nor humane. But, setting aside many practical difficulties which present themselves, the discussion of which would lead us too far from our principal object, it may, perhaps, be properly suggested that such removal is not even desirable. The negroes and white people of the South are adapted to each other. The antipathies of race, so strong in northern States, do not exist in the southern States, to nearly the same extent. The industry which sustains the whole population is supplied almost exclusively by negroes. Capitalists, being chiefly white people, are accustomed to direct and utilize this industry, and they are not accustomed to any other, and could not, for a generation, become thoroughly and advantageously accustomed to any other. Were the negroes at once removed, it would be economical to restore them, even at an equal expense. Immediate substitution of other laborers in their stead, would be difficult and almost impracticable; yet, to the people and their industrial interests, it would be depressing to spend a generation in the forced substitution of other laborers for negroes. The negroes would probably be subjected, during such a transition, to far greater hardships, neglect and abuse, than what ordinarily attend the condition of slavery. Especially would this be the case, under any system forced upon the people of a State by the United States Government. Better immediate and universal removal, and immediate substitution of

another system of labor, than the long agony of any transitional
system, coddled by external authority.

This brings us to a conclusion on this point, harmonizing with
the philosophical and practical excellence of our governmental
system, as it is. The people themselves should conduct their own
reforms. They may not even know, from time to time, more than
the first step in advance, but, taking that, the next becomes plainer.
That slavery is wrong, and ought at once everywhere to cease, all
can see: but the way out of it can best be found by those who
themselves have that way to travel. The United States Government ought not, in time of peace, to exercise jurisdiction in the
States over this subject; and no amendment to the Constitution,
giving to the General Government such jurisdiction, ought to
be made, if it could. Marring the principles and harmony of
the system by the introduction of an exceptional provision specially to reach slavery, would be, in itself, useless and mischievous; for the principle here insisted on is right, not because it is
in the Constitution, but it is in the Constitution because it is
right.

The principles, system and actual necessities of slavery have
been shown to be irreconcilable with our established constitutional
democratic republican system of government. We have seen that
our republican system must certainly be sustained; and the logical inference that slavery can not be, but must certainly pass
away, has been decidedly and unequivocally expressed in these
pages. But it seems also plain that the way in which it must
pass away, is through the voluntary action of the people of the
respective States where it exists; and that, save by example and
moral influence, the United States Government can best and most
effectively aid in the work, by confining itself faithfully to its
constitutional obligations of guaranteeing republicanism and
peace in every State, with the right of *habeas corpus*, and to
peaceably assemble and petition for redress of grievances, with
freedom of speech and of the press, so that the people thereof
may have fair opportunity — in the language of Mr. Calhoun, before given — "for the free and full operation of all the moral elements in favor of change." How great are the obligations laid
on the General Government to comply with these guarantees —
which it has too much neglected in the past — may be more fully
understood by reflecting that "the sacred right of revolution"

against oppressive government, which belongs to all men, is, in effect, nearly nullified as to the inhabitants of the respective States, by that other provision guaranteeing State governments against insurrection. These respective guaranties by the United States Government, are not merely absolute, but are also relative. As it commands and guarantees peace in every State, so also, by paramount obligation, must it guarantee republicanism to the inhabitants thereof, and the right and opportunity for free discussion, as their rightful means to relieve themselves from any oppression against which the right of revolution might be exercised, but for the interposition of the United States Government, in pursuance of its duty to guarantee peace. The free and full operation of the moral elements in favor of change, thus guaranteed to the people of the respective States, richly compensates for any abridgment of their right of revolution, by reason of the other guaranty; and, using again the language of Mr. Calhoun, with regard to these moral agencies, we add : "Nor ought their overpowering efficacy to accomplish the object intended, to be doubted. Backed by perseverance and sustained by these powerful auxiliaries, reason in the end will surely prevail over error and abuse, however obstinately maintained ; and this the more surely, by the exclusion of so dangerous an ally as mere brute force." Thus we see that no repetition, on a larger scale, of the scenes through which the slaves of St. Domingo became free, is necessary here, if we will but understand and use our excellent system of government: for it furnishes the sure means of dealing peacefully, yet effectively, with even so gigantic a social evil as slavery.

Let it not be inferred that a return is contemplated, to the condition on the subject of slavery, including the state of public opinion, which preceded this rebellion and war. This is neither possible nor desirable. Slavery, we repeat, must cease : and it must enter immediately into its process of cessation and disappearance from this entire land ; and immediately, from this time forth and forever, it must cease to dominate, or even to dictate, the course of the General Government. They who think otherwise, they who hope, and they who fear, that the incubus of slavery upon our political action and modes of thought, is to be replaced, do not know what has happened. The moral revolution in this respect, accomplished by the election of Mr. Lincoln, and sealed now by the blood shed in this rebellion to resist it, can not possibly be turned back. Every man in the nation who contributed to accomplish it, is, if possible, ten times more in earnest now to perpetuate it; and many, very many, of those who timidly or otherwise opposed it, would, with still more earnest zeal, now oppose a counter-revolution. The people of this country, with whatever prejudices they may enter upon any subject which they are compelled to consider, do gradually become educated in it; and the masses, having no permanent interest to go wrong, and led by their instincts, or a higher power, toward the right, do rest, finally, in wiser and juster conclusions. The one fact that they will never again consent to the restoration to the slave interest, of the control and management of the General Government, will be very effective to aid the downfall of slavery in the States. It will speedily dispose almost entirely of the most numerous and most mischievous class of men laboring to advance its interests — the men, namely, in all the States, free as well as slave, who, without having, perhaps, any direct interest in slavery, have, nevertheless, found its advocacy the reliable road to political preferment. This will soon leave to the people in the several States, only the actual slaveholders themselves to deal with. It will do more. It will raise up, in every slave State, on the side of republicanism, men who will engage openly in its support. It has been shown that from slaveholders themselves, as a class, nothing is to be hoped towards the voluntary relinquishment of slavery. But henceforth, in every State, the men who, from interest or principle, are opposed to slavery, must certainly be heard; and ere long, these will naturally and rightfully control every State, shape its policy, and enact its laws. Out of their own necessities and aspirations will the people of each State build themselves up.

Through the interested cupidity of the slaveholders, and the no less interested selfishness of their political advocates, inclining them to asperse those whom they have wronged, and through the groundless fears of the timid and the ignorant, the difficulties in the way of emancipation have undoubtedly been greatly exaggerated; and to these, we think, is chiefly owing the tendency to connect always with the idea of emancipation, some great and costly enterprise which deters people from the undertaking. A people who have demonstrated the folly of so many popular alarms, intended to repress development of different classes of men, and who have invariably found that every kind and class of men are made better, and not worse, by freedom, and by the recognition of all the common rights of humanity, ought not, so readily, to suppose that a rule which has always worked well, and never ill, will be totally reversed the moment it is applied to persons of African birth or descent. No State in which negroes are now free would be at all benefited, but, on the contrary, would be greatly injured, by reducing the negroes in it to slavery; and, according to the same principle, were the present slaves in any slave State emancipated, it would be a change for the worse, to restore the system of slavery. It is better for the people of any State, and for all of them, that the negroes who may be in it should be free, than that they should be enslaved. In other words, freedom is better than slavery for all men, and for all races and classes of men (except such as may have forfeited the right by crime), and it is better, also, for all with whom they may be, for a longer or a shorter time, in contact.

If these simple propositions are true, there can be no necessity for providing in advance an elaborate and costly system of colonization, or any other method of disposing of the negroes, before doing what is right in itself and advantageous to any State where they may be. Pertinent to this subject we quote here some suggestions which seem deserving of consideration, remarking, also, that their inherent force can not fairly be held any the less, because their author is of African descent, and has himself been for many years a slave:

"My answer to the question, what shall be done with the four million slaves, if emancipated? shall be short and simple. Do nothing with them, but leave them just as you leave other men, to do with and for themselves. We would be entirely respectful to those who raise this inquiry, and yet it is hard not to say to them just what they would say to us, if we manifested a like concern for them, and that is: please to mind your business and leave us to mind ours. If we can not stand up, then let us fall down. We ask nothing at the hands of the American people but simple justice, and an equal chance to live; and if we can not live and flourish on such terms, our case should be referred to the Author of our existence. Injustice, oppression and slavery, with all their manifold concomitants, have been tried with us during a period of more than two hundred years. Under the whole heavens you will find no parallel to the wrongs we have endured. We have worked without wages; we have lived without hope, wept without sympathy, and bled without mercy. Now, in the name of a common humanity, and according to the law of the Living God, we simply ask the right to bear the responsibility of our own existence." * * * * "Do nothing with us, for us, or by us, as a particular class. What you have done with us thus far has only worked to our disadvantage. We now simply ask to be allowed to do for ourselves. I submit that there is nothing unreasonable or unnatural in this request. The black man is said to be unfortunate. I affirm that the broadest of the black man's misfortunes is the fact that he is everywhere regarded and treated as an exception to the principles and maxims which apply to other men."

Jefferson said, "the world is governed too much." Is it not possible that much of the excessive anxiety to dispose of the negro, before recognizing his rights, is a part of this same error?

The slaves of the South enjoy advantages for information decidedly superior to those of the great majority of white people there, because of their contact with the educated whites, from which the poor whites (who can not read for themselves) are mostly excluded. This fact added to the other, above mentioned, that they perform nearly all the useful labor, may reasonably raise doubts, not only of the wisdom of their exportation, but of their being the best class to spare, in case all can not remain together.

Let it not be supposed that colonization, or any other enterprise, beneficial to the parties interested, and not morally wrong, is objected to. We are only insisting that such measures shall come in their proper way and order, and be adopted, if at all, because they are seen to be good, rather than because outsiders propose them. Good and useful measures ought not to be prejudiced by being awkwardly and rudely thrust forward. The same philosophical reason which makes it wiser and more practical for local governments to conduct local affairs, makes it wiser and more practical for the people who are themselves to be affected by any enterprise intended for their benefit, to be themselves engaged — not forcibly and sullenly, but spontaneously and cheerfully — in carrying it into effect.

Successful colonization is not only conceivable, but its contemplation may reasonably present pictures to warm the heart, and to kindle the imagination. But, if possible, let there be no exception to the rule, that the children whom our country may send forth from her teeming bosom to carry our arts and enterprise and civilization where they may be in demand, shall be led by a conscious affinity for their undertaking, and shall go forth, not as enemies, and with no envenomed stings rankling in their memories, to convert them into enemies.

It is not impossible that when the absolute necessity of emancipating the slaves shall be fully realized by the people of the slave States, they will themselves manifest unexpected wisdom and facility in devising how to do it easily; and also in disposing of that venerable stumbling block — what to do with the negroes? Indeed, it should hardly be matter of surprise if some of the most ultra advocates of slavery, and of a government adapted to it, should be prompt to labor for its speedy and entire removal and the thorough establishment of republicanism, when the rebellion and its objects shall have completely failed; or if some of the more southern slave States should thereupon take the lead in emancipation—if Texas, for instance, should leap forward, disenthralled, while Maryland, hugging her bonds, continues to sacrifice independent prosperity, for the doubtful benefits of a state of *betweenity*.

These views of the rationale of the crisis, are presented on the supposition of a rapid prosecution of the war to its natural conclusion. If it shall be so prosecuted, and the end accordingly reached ere long, or if, by an earlier and larger use of the national force, the end had been at any time heretofore reached, results, such as are here indicated, might, with reasonable confidence, be expected from the nature and character of our government and people, and the nature and character of the rebellion. In such case, the wisdom and propriety of making the restoration of the legitimate supremacy of the General Government throughout the land, the end and object of the war, would abundantly and satisfactorily appear. But the fundamental principles of slavery and of republicanism respectively, being such as have been described, their antagonism may, through modified circumstances, lead to modified results.

If, for instance, the conductors of our government, lacking confidence in the practical excellence of our governmental system, should, in any manner whatever, compromise this rebellion, or again attempt to commit the General Government in any manner whatever to the support of slavery, the irrepressible conflict between its real principles and those of slavery might be indefinitely protracted, to culminate, possibly, in results very different from such as are here foreshadowed. So obvious, however, is the unwisdom of such course, and so improbable its adoption, that it is dismissed without consideration.

Another possible course is not so entirely improbable, and, therefore, deserves some attention. In ordinary contests, where

numbers of men have become engaged in hostility, even in deadly
hostility, a spirit of conciliation and kindness manifested by one
side, acts favorably upon the other, and prepares both for acquiescence in reasonable and amicable relations. But this is where
— as in most contests among men — a misunderstanding is at the
bottom of the difficulty, and reconciliation is easy when passion
is subdued. In the present case, the real difficulty becomes more
irreconcilable the better it is understood. It is, as has been shown,
a contest of irreconcilable principles. The principles on one side
harmonize with, and are incorporated into, our system of government; those on the other must, if allowed to prevail, overthrow
our system of government. For the sake of peace, too far, already, has been carried the attempt to acquiesce in their joint
recognition; but. in the nature of the case, their joint control was
impossible. The arbitrament of force became a necessity; hence,
conciliation and kindness have, in this case, failed of their usual
efficacy. But conciliation and kindness, on the part of our
Government, are perseveringly tried, as though it were still hoped
that these can be substituted for force. This necessarily protracts
the war.

Slavery, the common interest which provoked the rebellion,
unites and controls, in a consolidated whole, all the men and
means throughout the disaffected territory, in the same manner
and by the same necessity, described in our earlier pages, in relation to the control of State governments in slave States. State
rights, used as a pretext to start the rebellion, are no longer necessary, and are not now heard of in rebeldom. any more than
popular rights, or democratic principles; but all governmental
agencies are, in effect, consolidated and wielded by the power
which raises and controls their armies. That power is perfectly
inaccessible through conciliation and kindness. The people for
whom these are intended, are not reached and can not be reached
by them, till that power is beaten down, and with it the barriers
of prejudice and hatred which it has raised so high and strengthened so broadly.

That power will never voluntarily submit to the restoration of
the legitimate supremacy of our republican government. It says
so, emphatically and continually, and it is time to believe that,
in this, it says truly. Not unreasonably, perhaps, does it calculate on the continuance, and possibly the increase, of the anxiety

to conciliate, with the protraction of the war; and it hopes for all the chances which might still render possible the attainment of its object. Days and months as they pass, accustom to its sway the people whom it can reach; and while this power is embodied anywhere in a State, the United States Government can only hold by its superior power any territory in the State. But it has been shown that the United States Government can not properly lend itself to the support of slavery. It is not, theoretically or constitutionally, a slaveholding government, and, by abolishing slavery wherever it has the power, it is harmonizing its practices with its principles. It can not properly make the temporary administration of local government in States an exception; and thus, any State law of slavery, is, for the time, in abeyance during the administration of local government in a slave State by the United States Government, under military necessity. Not, therefore, by any direct act of the United States Government abolishing slavery in the States, but simply by neglect and refusal to administer the State law, slavery lacks enforcement where the armies of the Union go. If this continues, slavery rapidly dies. It is not probable that this result has been contemplated as one of policy; but it is not the less sure. Its poetic justice might suggest the idea of design; but we can not safely pursue justice in this way. Its cost is too enormous, and its results can better be obtained in the direct and normal way. War is not the business of this people, and it should not be permitted to become such, even for the sake of thereby suffocating slavery. The volunteers enlisted in military service should, as soon as possible, become peaceful and industrious citizens. Their officers should cease to exercise arbitrary authority, and the people should again become the dispensers of patronage. The General Government should, as soon as may be, cease to direct all the public energies, and the States should resume their relative significance and importance. Great as would be the future benefit to the country and to mankind, if slavery in the States were extinguished, protracted war, with its centralizing tendencies, its enormous expense, its demoralization, its alienation, its sufferings, bereavements and desolations, is too much to pay for the accomplishment of such purpose; especially when this desired result is so sure to follow the restoration of the legitimate supremacy of the General Government, guaranteeing peace and republicanism throughout the land; a result, let us re-

7

peat, that is by none so well understood as by those who initiated this rebellion on purpose to escape it.

A continued guerrilla warfare by the minions of slavery is not to be apprehended from the omission to extinguish slavery by United States force. The organized forces of the rebellion are what now sustain such guerrilla warfare, wherever it exists ; and when the armies of slavery shall be overcome and dispersed, and its *quasi* national organization annihilated, the people of the several States, through their State Governments, sustained by the General Government, will easily dispose of guerrillas. It will plainly be for their interest to do so. State Governments are in no respect dangerous or unfriendly to our General Government ; but the only real and considerable dangers proceed from combinations, extending through many States, and assuming to oppose or to usurp the functions of the General Government. When the rebellious Confederacy that slavery has organized, shall be entirely overcome and extinguished, the rebellion itself will be ended, and the legitimate supremacy of the General Government be reëstablished throughout the land.

This idea brings into view the exceeding folly of the proposition sometimes suggested, from ignorant or unfriendly sources, of an armistice, negociation, or compromise with the hostile power. The very source of all the difficulty is in the mere existence of such hostile power. To negociate with it or to recognize it in any way whatever, is to sanction the greatest possible political evil. No political power has a right to exist here for one moment, save the States and the General Government ; and the only way towards peace is the complete annihilation and disappearance of any such pretended intermediary power. It can not exist one moment after the legitimate supremacy of the General Government is reëstablished throughout the land ; and the moment this is done, there is peace.

It is, therefore, so simple as to seem but the repetition of an identical proposition, to conclude — as we unhesitatingly do, after this review of all essential suggestions on the subject — that *the proper end and object of the war is the restoration of the legitimate supremacy of the General Government throughout the land.*

Not only does this method commend itself to our judgment, but we see that it is the one designed by the fathers of the republic. It has only failed hitherto in certain respects, because of our culpable neglect to apply our republican principles. Attempting to be wise above what was written, and trusting to expedients rather than to principles, we have cultivated disaffection into rebellion and civil war. Are we not justly punished for our political sins? Our system of government as it is, is competent, not only for the present emergency, but for all future emergencies which now seem likely to arise; and the suggestions to amend it, as though it were mechanical machinery which wears out, instead of being, as it is, a philosophical application of eternal principles, originate, not in the wisdom of statesmanship, but in the temporizing plans of political expediency. Let us elevate ourselves to the comprehension and management of this most excellent and beautiful system. It is intended and adapted for the people's use. Discussion and agitation should not be avoided. They are always and everywhere the necessary attendants of wise deliberation. Adopting again the language of Mr. Calhoun: "They are indispensible means, the only school (if I may be allowed the expression) in our case, that can diffuse and fix in the mind of the community the principles and duties necessary to uphold our complex but beautiful system of governments. In none that ever existed are they so much required; and in none were they ever calculated to produce such powerful effect."

As our Government is good, so are our circumstances, in some most important respects, propitious.

Not accidentally, but designedly, the American people have now, as the executive head of their General Government, a man of honest purpose, logical mind, and such firmness as requires not the aid of wordy demonstration. If cautious and conciliatory, he is also true. He is not stationary, like the Bourbons, but progressive, like Channing, because, in spite of conservative tendencies in his political education, he believes in principles, and fears not to follow where he sees they lead. Some, who have praised him as conservative, may yet be shocked by his radicalism; and some, who think him slow, may find themselves astonished at his advance. For ourselves, we believe that his course of administration, as it proceeds, will prove a new illustration of the old truth: "The path of the just is as the shining light, that shineth more and more unto the perfect day."

Our people are now showing themselves worthy of their government and of their destiny. Suppressing, by their united and almost omnipotent power, the violence that would not submit to reason, they are, while in this performance of a home duty, subduing, also, the prejudices of a world. That respect, which attends the exhibition of gigantic national power, gives us new security for national peace. The revival of republicanism among ourselves encourages its revival everywhere,

> "and our hopes
> Go forward to the glorious train of years,
> When all the clouds of strife that darken earth
> And hide the face of heaven, shall roll away ;
> And like a calm, sweet sunshine, peace and love
> Shall light the drearest walks of human life."

www.ingramcontent.com/pod-product-compliance
Lightning Source LLC
Chambersburg PA
CBHW022344020726
47500CB00004B/1268